Dirty Words
stories

Todd Robinson

DIRTY WORDS: stories
ISBN-13: 978-1480074873
ISBN-10: 148007487X
Copyright 2012
All stories ©Todd Robinson

Published by THUGLIT Publishing

Table of Contents

Todd Robinson

An Introduction, George Lucas-ing, and a Confession...

Hello there.

Name's Todd Robinson.

Not sure what else to go with by way of introduction...

Some of you (I would assume most of you who dropped coin on the collection in the first place) might have some idea who I am. If you don't, good luck and God bless.

If you DO know me, it's probably through the website THUGLIT that I created and edited for five years (and its subsequent anthologies). Maybe you've seen one or more of my stories floating around the web or in one of the publications that have blessed me with acceptance over the years.

Or maybe I just harangued you into buying the fucking thing while you were sitting at the bar.

Yeah, I'm a bartender. That means that you'll see some connective tissues between the stories other than characters. Write what you know. I know bars, the people who work there, the people who drink there. The damaged souls, the weirdos, the characters, the alcoholics, junkies, the lonely, and everybody in between. I love these people, warts and all. I consider some of the most damaged my friends. I hope that by the end of these stories, you will too.

Either way, thanks for being here. All monies derived go to a couple of good causes. First of which are the goddamn cat's medical bills. For the record? The cat is dead. His bills aren't.

The second is taking my kid to Disneyland for the first time.

Hey, I said good causes, I never said charity. And if dead cats and taking nice kids to Disneyland don't qualify as good causes to you, you're probably a prick.

So there...

Where were we?

Oh yeah. Introductions.

At this point, you might be thinking that I'm a prick, what with the previous paragraphs and all, blah, blah, blah. I wouldn't disagree with you. If that's the case, buckle up, Buttercup, because the stories you got coming are no more pleasant than I am.

So if you normally spend your hard-earned loot on crime stories that feature a nice scone recipe, you might as well stop right here. It ain't gonna get any better for you.

I won't take it personally; hell, my mother agrees with you. However, long as you're not like my mother, you might dig what lies ahead. Hope you do.

George Lucas-ing

In the grand tradition of Mr. Lucas (and running the risk of fucking it all up), not all of the stories collected here are as they were when originally printed. Like most writers, I couldn't resist the urge to tweak the prose, correct some questionable phrasings, and sometimes just flat-out change shit. For instance, two separate characters in two different stories had the same first name. In order to maintain an even flow between stories, one of them had to adopt a sudden alias.

HOWEVER, there was one story that required a drastic facelift. The story was fine, the characters and dialogue worked, but some of the prose was just awful. I mean…just really awful. It was an early published tale, and I'm glad and grateful that it got picked up, but for the life of me, I have no idea how somebody thought it was overall fit to print.

So, if you notice some changes between a story you may have read before and one collected here and it bugs you, seriously…you need a hobby.

A Confession (or two)

Before I get a bunch of angry e-mails from those of you who read HARDCORE HARDBOILED, the first of the THUGLIT anthologies, I'm Sam Edwards.

Lemme explain.

When I first started the website, we didn't have enough submissions for the first issue. I mean, we did, but for some reason, we got a shitload of stories that didn't necessarily fit our bill. Yeah, that's a nice story about visiting your grandfather's grave in Argentina, but what in sweet fuck-all does it have to do with crime fiction?

You get my point.

I was committed to getting the first issue up, but lo and behold, I didn't have enough material. So I dusted off "The Long Count", one of my trunk stories, and threw it up under Sam Edwards (Sam and Edward being the first names of my grandfathers). I didn't tell my other editors.

Then the dang thing gets selected by BEST AMERICAN MYSTERY STORIES as a "Notable Story of the Year".

I kept my mouth shut. The biggest honor of my short writing career, and I couldn't tell anybody. THAT kinda sucked.

Then, when Kensington books decided to print our anthologies, of course they insisted that I include all of the award-nominated/winning stories.

I decided to get clever.

Sam Edward's bio reads:

Truly other digests deserving recognition on bios, instead, Nasty Sam offers nothing.

Now, take the first letter in each word…

Yeah, nobody figured it out then either. I only spent about three days writing out the acrostic. Time well spent, no?

Oh, and if you actually bought any copies and had the book signed at an event by Sam? That was really Julius Franco, my best friend and co-conspirator in all of life's misadventures since the age of thirteen.

Aaaaaaand some of you may recognize the THUGLIT story (and Derringer-nominated short) "Roses at his Feet" as written by Ms. Dana Frittersmash.

Uh, yeah. I'm her, too.

Again, if you've already read that one, I'm reeeeeeally sorry. But hey, you still got nine more stories here!

Lemme explain (again…)

After the first issue, I hard-marketed the website online and at BoucherCon, the annual crime writing festival. For issues two and three, I was FLOODED with submissions.

Issue four? Sahara. Still managed to put a great issue together.

Then, two days before we were set to launch the issue, a writer inexplicably pulled his piece (this is also why that cover is so shitty and slapped-together-looking). In response, I panicked, made a pot of coffee and stayed up all night writing the story.

The next morning, seeking a new pen name, I accidentally stepped on the apple fritter my wonderful wife had brought me while watching the previous night's UFC interview with Dana White.

Bada-bing, bada-boom, Dana Frittersmash.

Next thing I know, THAT story is nominated for a Derringer.

Although I have to admit that I did emit a few chuckles when I read the letter from the Derringer committee asking for Ms. Frittersmash's contact info.

Again, whoopsie.

And that was that. I never wrote another story under a pen name, although I should, considering the amount of accolades my alter-egos receive.

Maybe my reputation precedes me...

ENJOY, FUCKO!

So Long, Johnnie Scumbag

Johnnie sat behind the glass partition in his prison oranges, huffing a Newport. Obese, pale and tired-looking, jail hadn't been kind to him. Not that it's particularly kind to anybody. His dyed black hair was starting to show its brown roots, giving his head a layered chocolate cake look. Johnnie smelled bad to begin with, but the stint in lock-up wasn't doing his hygiene any favors. It might have been my imagination, but I could have sworn that I could smell him through the inch and a half of plexiglass. I tried to cover his stink of garlic mixed with wet dog by chain smoking, until the guard informed me of the no smoking policy.

Christ. Can't even smoke in jail. I wondered what the hell passed for currency on the yard since 2003.

I'd just have to breathe through my mouth then. What I needed was a drink. As it was, I interrupted my day's barflying to see Johnnie in the first place.

"T.C., I need you on this, man," he said. Not that he didn't cut a pathetic picture to begin with, but his blubbering only made him seem fatter. Maybe it was my own word association with blubber.

"Tell me why I should, Johnnie."

"'Cause I didn't do this!"

"Again Johnnie, tell me why I should give a shit." I wanted an answer and I wanted it fast. I didn't enjoy being at Riker's, even if it was a friend in there. And in case you didn't have it figured out by now, I'm not a big fan of

Johnnie Scumbag's. Nobody really is. The people who *like* him call him Johnnie Scumbag.

"Because I don't have a lot of time and you're the only person who can do it."

I wasn't, but I was probably the only one who'd shown up when Johnnie called. My services, no matter how mundane, don't come cheap. In the sudden economic slide in New York City, jobs had been so scarce lately that I was even willing to show up for Johnnie Scumbag. Most people who would've been clients a year ago tried to do their own work instead in order to save a few bucks. Most of them wound up on Johnnie's side of the glass. If they were lucky.

"Convince me with a number," I said.

"Five grand," Johnnie said, hopefully.

"Six." I tried to keep my feet from fidgeting in my shoes. Jail gives me the heebie-jeebies. Probably because something deep inside told me that I would end up in one eventually.

"Why six?"

"Jeannie Giammarino told me to remind you that you owe her a grand off the last Klitchko fight."

"What, she think I was gonna welsh?" Johnnie puffed his chest out in a pose of dignified disbelief.

"The fight was in January. She's been waiting five months."

"I was getting the money together."

"Yeah. And the check's in the mail." He spoke to me as if I didn't know him and his history. The nickname "scumbag" wasn't put on people known for their high standards of integrity.

Johnnie didn't like my attitude. "Then maybe you should help me because I know what you *really* do, T.C." He flashed a smirk that I wanted to peel off with a lemon zester.

I let his words hang for a bit. I felt a smile play across my own mouth. "You threatening me, Johnnie?" My words were ice. My look was colder.

Johnnie quickly reconsidered his tactic. "No, no T.C., I...I mean...I know you can help me." Beads of sweat popped out on his face. "That little bastard Tino's setting me up."

I sucked in my upper lip. "Tino's girlfriend is dead. Seems to me like a damned stupid way to be setting you up."

"The guy gets robbed, see? He lives on Sullivan Street, for chrissakes. There's a junkie every ten feet since they got shoo-flyed out of Washington Square. He tells the cops it was me and here I am."

Truth was, despite everything else that made him a piece of shit, Johnnie was no killer.

Fuck it. I needed income.

"Give me the names."

The deal.

Tino, one of the last people in the Tri-State area who had any faith in Johnnie, let him stay with him a bit while he was "between apartments." I'd be more likely to believe that if Johnnie ever had an address for more than a couple months at a time. He'd attach himself like a tick to someone until they wizened up and changed their locks. Problem was, Johnnie's few possessions were still in Tino's after his keys stopped working. Up to that point, everyone else had returned Johnnie's stuff if only to guarantee his absence from their lives. Tino thought differently. Johnnie was going to pay him back all of the money he owed or else his stuff would hit the furnace. Then Tino comes home one night to find his girlfriend Nina dead on the floor, the apartment robbed down to the hardwood.

Nina was four months pregnant.

Johnnie claimed that he'd been playing poker in Williamsburg the whole night. Problem was, the game was illegal and nobody wanted to admit having been there. Even if they were, fewer were willing to step up to the plate for Johnnie Scumbag.

My first stop was Paulie D's Barbershop. It was a nice day, so I took the L train into Brooklyn and walked up Metropolitan to Paulie's.

A tin bell tinkled as I walked in. "How's things Paulie?"

Paulie didn't bother looking up. He was busy sweeping up a mess of curly blonde hair off the floor. Paulie looked like a shaved ferret, only slightly taller. A shaved ferret with a horrible personality. In the dingy back room of the dingier barbershop, he ran illegal poker games on weekends for the gambling junkies who didn't want to bother getting a bus to Atlantic City.

Paulie just grunted at me. The fresh hair told me that somebody new was in the neighborhood. Anybody who'd lived there more than a week knew that the barbershop was a front and wouldn't trust Paulie to shear a sheep, much less cut their hair—not unless they wanted to look like Patti LaBelle after she'd stuck her head in a thresher. Most people of reasonable intelligence just had to look at the magazine rack to figure it out. His most recent copy of Sports Illustrated featured Johnnie Bench on the cover.

"Hey Paulie, was Johnnie Scumbag at poker on Saturday?"

"Polka? I don't know nothin' about no Polack dancing."

I could see I was going to be on the receiving end of Paulie's legendary talent for playing dumb. "The poker game. P-O-K-E-R."

"What poker game?"

"The one on Saturday."

"What's poker?"

I sighed. I should have known better. If push came to shove, Paulie would wind up with his own ass in a sling if he gave Johnnie his alibi. "This is between you and me, Paulie. I just need to know whether or not he was here."

Paulie stopped sweeping and gave me the once over. "Why you wanna know?"

"He's in Riker's for something that went down on Saturday night and he needs somebody to say that he was elsewhere."

"It ain't gonna be me."

"Well, I need to know."

Paulie scratched his chin. "He came by Saturday night. Got his hair cut."

That was all I needed to hear. Johnnie wouldn't let Paulie touch his hair with a velvet glove, much less his scissors. "How long?"

"He was here all night. Man's got one helluva complicated haircut."

"Would you be willing to tell a cop that? Even on the DL"

"Nope." Paulie resumed his sweeping. I started to leave when the broom stopped. "Next time you see that fat turd, you tell him he dropped one of his cards under his chair when he left."

"*His* cards?"

"Wasn't one of mine. You tell him he comes back again, I'm gonna cut more than his hair."

I left Brooklyn and returned to Manhattan for stop number two over at Dino's bar.

Josh already had the bottle of Makers in his hand when I told him I was having coffee. The bottle hovered for a second in Josh's unbelieving hand.

"Seriously?"

"Seriously. I'm working."

"Whew! For a second I thought you were gonna say you were on the wagon. I don't think I make my rent, you stop drinking."

"Hardy har, Sheckie."

Josh poured me a cup that tasted like it was brewed around the time Paulie picked up that Johnnie Bench S.I.

Scumbag claimed that Josh was at the poker game with him. Or danced a polka with him. After my talk with Paulie, I wasn't so sure anymore. After my tongue stopped shitting in my mouth from that first sip of coffee, I said as much.

"What poker game?" Josh said innocently. Or as innocently as a man sleeved in tattoos with an old bottle scar across one cheek can say it.

"Don't start that shit with me, Josh. I just went through it with Paulie." Josh and I went back a-ways together, so I wasn't about to play verbal hide & seek with him. I'd been a semi-regular at Dino's for a decade and tip well for an alcoholic. The amount of money I'd dropped in the last year alone should have been enough to buy me some straight talk.

"Okay, okay. Yeah. I was there. So was Scumbag."

"He's gonna need somebody to alibi him then."

Josh shook his head. "I'm not doing it. My wife finds out I was gambling, she's gonna have my balls in her spaghetti sauce."

I accidentally slugged another mouthful of coffee. Josh reached for the pot to refill it and I almost pulled my gun. "So don't say you were gambling. Say you were at a bar with him. Say you were playing pool with him. Say you were dancing a goddamn cha-cha with him in Monte Carlo for all I fucking care."

Josh blushed a deep red all the way up to the tips of his ears. "I can't"

"Why the hell not?"

"Well..." The red deepened into crimson. "My wife doesn't know I was out. I kinda snuck out after she fell asleep. She takes an Ambien, she wouldn't notice if I had the poker game in the bed on top of her."

"Josh, an innocent man is in jail right now and you're willing to let him stay there because you're afraid of your wife?"

"You never met Janelle, have you?"

"No…"

"There you go."

"For the love of…"

"And you got a weird sense of humor calling Johnnie Scumbag innocent." Josh's face went hard when he said it.

I met his eyes evenly. "He didn't rob Tino, Josh. If he was with you at the poker game, he didn't kill Nina either. Or the baby."

"Yeah. I know all about that. It's a tragedy. But Johnnie ain't no saint, either."

"I know that."

Josh nodded, solemnly. "You know about Geraldine?"

The name sounded familiar, but a face wouldn't appear in my mind. "I think so. What about her?"

"You mighta called her Sharkie."

"Oh yeah, Sharkie." Sharkie was a local hustler who fleeced the uptown boys whenever they played pool on the L.E.S. She wasn't a supremely skilled player, but was extremely gifted, nonetheless. Gifted by the way of 38-24-36, two inches of tits more than the Commodores granted. She played in a wifebeater t-shirt and a pair of bike shorts. Looking like she did, the best pool players in the world had trouble lining up a shot while staring at her womanly goodness. To top it all off, she possessed both a smile and nature so sweet, her marks would lose all of their money and then break out credit cards to buy her drinks when she was done. "What's this got to do with Sharkie?" I asked. "She hasn't been around in a while."

Josh made a face like he'd drank some of his own coffee. "You can thank Johnnie Scumbag."

"What are you talking about?"

"About a year and a half ago, she was in here and had a bit too much." Josh made the drinky-drinky motion. "She left with Scumbag."

"Sharkie left with Scumbag?" I couldn't keep the horror out of my voice.

"Yeah, I know. Some people are inclined to believe that she was slipped something a little harder than alcohol, if you know what I'm saying."

I didn't say anything.

"Anyway," Josh continued, "Six months pass and Sharkie's heavy with kid. Tells Scumbag he's the poppa. I mean, Sharkie was a standup broad. She didn't cry foul or nothin', just said to Scumbag that the baby was his. Scumbag pulls his innocent act and disappears on her. How much money do you think the kid's seen from him so far?"

I didn't say anything again. The answer was obvious. I knew Sharkie and I knew Scumbag. There was no defense. I felt like an armless boxer fighting for the heavyweight title.

"Exactly. So don't come preaching to me about poor, innocent Johnnie Scumbag." Josh clicked his tongue in disgust. "And if that don't beat all, the fucking kid's gotta look just like Scumbag. Couldn't look like Sharkie, could it? What a fucking world."

I was down to bare knuckles. Last resorting for a man I didn't even like. I already felt covered in the film of slime that Johnnie Scumbag seemed to leave wherever he went. But I did it anyway. I went to talk to Tino.

We met at a bar on the corner of Sullivan and Houston. I remembered the place as a biker bar twenty years ago. Now the place was a lounge. Progress, I suppose. Tino looked off into the south Manhattan skyline when I brought our drinks over. He swallowed hard twice before he seemed capable of drinking his beer. Tino was a small man made downright miniscule by pain. His grief was a palpable thing that he wore around his neck like an anchor in a world rapidly filling with water.

I broke the quiet moment. "Johnnie didn't do it, Tino."

Tino nodded. "Then I will find out who did." The last remaining touches of his Spanish accent flicked across his words like a feather.

"You can tell the cops that you found out. That he didn't do it."

He nodded again, more to himself than to me. "Don't care."

"Tino…" I didn't know how to finish the sentence, so I didn't.

"I wasn't home. I took an extra night at work to cover the money that cocksucker Johnnie took from us. I would have been home if not for him. I could have protected my wife. My baby."

"You don't know what would have happened, Tino."

"Or I could have died with them. Even that would have been better." Tino cleared his throat hard.

We sat in the leaded quiet for a time. Tino's watery eyes never left the darkening skyline. "Did you know it was a boy?"

Two days passed before I met up with Johnnie Scumbag again.

"You know what an all-region DVD player is?"

Johnnie gave me a look through the plexiglass like I'd lost my mind. "I know what a DVD player is."

I shook my head. "When they first started making the players, they made them all-region. Which means that if you wanted to watch a movie that was only available in French Polynesia, you could. Then the companies figured out that if they made machines that only played the region in which they were bought, that they could sell more. That way if anyone moved from one county to another, they'd not only have to buy a new player, but all new DVDs as well. Also, depending on what country makes what movie, different release dates, etc, etc... Sometimes a movie will already out on DVD in one country before it's in theaters in another."

Johnnie continued staring at me, puzzled. "And?"

"And, Tino had one of those models."

"I don't know what..."

"You see, Johnnie, Tino loves kung-fu movies. He's loved them since he was a kid. He collects them. Problem was, a lot of the movies he wanted were only made for the Chinese region. Are you following me?"

Johnnie nodded, mutely.

"So Tino goes out and he buys himself one of these all-region DVD players and orders the movies from Chinatown. Thing is, these machines are kinda rare nowadays. Only the hardcore guys own them and pay top dollar. So, a stolen one is easy to track."

"Uh-huh."

I pulled a cigarette out, placed it between my lips, feeling more than a little like Columbo. The guard "ahem"-med at me.

"Not lighting it," I said, a little pissed that my Columbo flow was now fucked up. "Where was I?"

"DVD player?"

"Ah, right. So, I hit the pawn shops. Sure enough, right on Sixth Avenue, less than a half mile from Tino's apartment, I find myself a pawn shop. Beginner's luck, I guess. Know what they had?"

Johnnie blinked at me, thinking it over and taking longer than he should. "Tino's DVD player?"

"Atta boy! You are following. Now, the pawn shop guy, he would never admit to buying stolen goods, much less give me a name or tell me that he buys the goods from the local junkies." I chewed the filter and smiled as I blew the pretend smoke slowly out my nostrils. "But it's amazing what they will tell you when you break out the cigar cutter and a can of Sterno."

Johnnie nodded silently as the color dropped out of his face between heartbeats.

I let him stew for a few seconds. "I found Chauncy, Johnnie."

"I didn't..."

"A couple of twenties passed into a junkie's hand and they'll tell you that they like to hump pumpkins, much less point a finger atanother junkie." I stubbed out the cigarette I never lit in the metal ashtray still bolted to the table.

"I didn't rob Tino, T.C. I didn't kill Nina," Johnnie's voice was starting to squeak with panic.

"No. No you didn't. You just paid Chauncey to break in and rob the place to get all your stuff back. Nina walked in and he killed her."

"I never meant..."

"You cut a path. Johnnie. Everywhere you go. Everything you touch leaves behind the stink of you. And I'm not just talking about that Fulton Fish Market at high noon aroma that comes out your pores, either."

Johnnie hung his head in...what? I don't know. Who knows if a person like him can feel shame. Or guilt. If I had the money to bet, I'd say that he hung his head in simple defeat at being found out. "What are you going to do?"

"Oh, there's a lot I could do. I could drop Chauncey off at the police station and let him confess, which at worst gets you an accessory charge."

Johnnie raised his head, hopeful.

"But that's not gonna happen since poor Chauncy is being sent to a few different states right now. All of them at the same time, if you catch my drift." I winked at him.

Johnnie went another shade whiter and his lower lip started to tremble. "But I didn't..."

"Yes you did, Johnnie. Yes you fucking did." I stabbed my finger at him. "Another option is Josh." I pulled a piece of paper out of my pocket. "The poor guy's conscience worked him over and at the risk of his horrible wife's fury, he wrote out a statement saying he was playing poker with you all Saturday night. Look." I held the paper up to the glass. "Even had it notarized." Johnnie's face pressed against the barrier, a sly smile pulling the corner of his mouth as he read Josh's words. The smile winked out when I tore the paper in two.

"No! *NO!*" he screamed, fat fingers trying to reach through the holes to get the shreds.

"Oops."

Deflated, Johnnie's face went slack, his eyes deadened at the realization that he wasn't going any-goddamn-where.

I turned to go and stopped, living out one last fine point of my Columbo fantasy. "One last thing," I said and turned back. "You remember Crazy Dennis? Used to run errands for the Westies way back?"

Johnnie tried to swallow and looked like he might vomit instead. "I think so. He got that teardrop tattoo on the corner of his eye?"

"Yup. That's him. He was supposedly the only guy crazy enough to actually give somebody a Columbian Necktie after he'd kill him. And if you were considered crazy in Hell's Kitchen mob back in those days… Anyway, funny thing. He got pulled over last week in Queens and the cops found an unregistered gun. He's getting two years in here on weapons possession. Strange when you think that's what they catch him for after all of the sick shit that Crazy Dennis pulled. Funny too, when you remember that his wife was Nina's sister." I savored the fear that fluttered in Johnnie's eyes. "Small world, ain't it, Johnnie?"

If Johnnie went any paler, he'd have gone invisible. He shook like an epileptic. His mouth moved, but no words came out. I turned to go, for real this time. I lifted my hand in farewell. "So long, Johnnie. Won't be seeing you."

The Biggest Dick In Brooklyn

"Pull yer pants down."

Over the course of the last thirty years, Henry DeMarco had given a lot of orders—a lot of strange and tough orders. For thirty years, nobody ever questioned their boss' demands until he walked into his warehouse and said those four bewildering words.

"What?" Scrawny little Pete Marino stopped his game of solitaire, the cards frozen in his hand.

Bobby Russo looked up from his Kubrick biography, but didn't move. Gino Bendetti just looked confused. Bobby translated. *"Lui vuole che caliamo i nostri pantaloni."*

"Che cosa?"

"I said, pull yer pants down!" Henry bellowed.

Bobby just shook his head, never taking his eyes off of his boss. Without another word, he stood and unbuckled his belt. Taking their cues off of Bobby, the other two followed suit.

He stands behind her at the bottom of her bed. She is face down, naked. Even in the dim light, every outline, every aspect of her body is in sharp contrast. The curves of her hips arch under the contours of her ass, the skin as smooth as dunes of white sand. The handcuffs cinching her wrists rattle on the metal bedposts. Her ankles are also chained to opposite posts at the foot of the large bed. She moans through the gag. She's completely helpless.

"Underwear too." DeMarco cinched his baby-blue bathrobe tight. In the past couple of months, the old boss hadn't bothered to dress himself properly, walking around the neighborhood in his worn robe and slippers. Questions arose about the quality of the man's sanity. The conversation they were currently having did nothing to assuage the doubts his own crew were having of late.

The three men stood side by side. Bobby in his boxers, Pete in his decades-old looking tighty whities. Unfortunately for them all, Gino still wore his Italian man-thong, his fashion sense apparently acclimating itself to Americana about as fast as his language skills.

Gino looked confused, but not as embarrassed as the other two. He looked to Bobby for another translation.

"Biancheria intima, pure." Bobby's expression was still blank.

Gino's face blanched. His Italian rattled off his tongue too fast for Bobby to translate. *"E' uno sherzo? Per quale motivo? In nome di Dio, che succede qui?"*

DeMarco's face reddened in rage. He couldn't understand Gino even when he wasn't going a mile a minute. What he did understand was his tone. "Bobby, you tell that fucking greenhorn to shut his yap and just do what I say. Lose the banana hammock."

Bobby nodded. *"Calmati, fai. Quello che dice, dopo vediamo."*

"Madre de dio," Gino muttered.

Pete looked like he wanted to cry. "Henry, please…"

"Pete, I swear to God…"

Bobby recognized the edge in his boss' voice. Whatever the fuck was bouncing around inside Henry DeMarco's head at that moment was deadly serious. At least to DeMarco. "Just do it, Pete," Bobby said in a calm voice he normally reserved for big dogs that have stopped wagging their tails. Bobby hooked his fingers into the elastic waistband of his drawers and dropped trou.

Just like his boss ordered.

He's watching her writhe in the cuffs. Her long red hair flows between her straining shoulders like a waterfall of blood. She knows what's going to happen next.

He pulls his t-shirt over his head, tossing it to the floor. Then he slowly unbuttons his pants. He's ready. In a minute, she will be, too.

He can't believe it's come to this, what he has to do on this night. He can't believe it, but he knows he has to.

A bead of sweat rolls down the side of her leg.

Henry chuckled at chicken-legged Pete, his bony ankles shaking in his Fruit of the Looms. "What the fuck is that, Petey? You smuggling pecans?"

"C'mon, Henry. It's cold in here," Pete whined.

"Pull your pants back up, Needledick Bugfucker."

Pete scrambled to pull his underwear and chinos back over what was left of his dignity. "That ain't right, Henry. Why you gotta make fun?"

DeMarco moved down to Gino and shook his head in disbelief. "Whaaat the fuck? How old is this guy?"

Che cosa sta chiedendo? Gino asked.

Vuole sapere la vostra eta'.

Gino smiled, finally able to answer a question in English all on his own. "I'm-a tirty-a-two." He grinned ear to ear, proud of himself despite the fact that he was standing with his tackle in the wind.

"Then why the fuck don't he have no pubes?"

"Che?"

"Mai mente." Bobby nearly cracked a smile despite himself. Bobby didn't know if was a European thing or not, but Gino apparently walked with his own code of international grooming as well.

"Jesus fuck," said DeMarco. "Tell Bald Eagle to beat it."

"Potete andare," Bobby said.

"Non dovete dirmelo due volte." With that, Gino quickly hustled his own pants back up to a respectable level and high-tailed out the door right behind Pete.

Bobby would have to thank them both later for leaving him alone with his nutbag boss and his nutbag out.

DeMarco stared at Bobby's crotch in silence for a long uncomfortable moment. Well, long and uncomfortable for Bobby, at least.

"Uhhhhh…Boss?"

DeMarco then clapped his hands and laughed heartily, like his grandkids had just run into the room on Christmas morning. "Hey, hey, Bob-BEE. Now *that's* what I'm talkin' about."

He kneels on the bed behind her and smells her hair—Chanel. Nice. She tenses when he places his hands on her hips. A quick mewl escapes from the gag. His heart thuds in excitement. He takes himself in his hand, positioning…

Bobby Russo knew he had a big dick from when he was thirteen and compared himself to the dudes on his Pop's porno videos. He didn't know exactly how much bigger until he started playing sports and had to shower with the other boys.

Then he realized he was fucking huge.

When John Holmes died, the other guys used to joke that Bobby was in first place now.

For all he knew, he was.

On the bus, Bobby always tried to get the seat next to Loretta Delveccio since Loretta had a bad habit of falling asleep on the ride to school. When she started snoring, Bobby would open his pants and place his dick on her lap while his buddies (who couldn't even get their dicks onto their own laps) nearly herniated themselves trying not to laugh. Yeah, Bobby's dick had served him well over the years, not only sexually, but as a comedy prop.

But he never realized that it could be used as a weapon.

"He wants you to do what?" Pete's mouth hung open. Three scotches later and his hands still shook from the ordeal.

"He told me to fuck Angela."

"Angela?"

"Angela." Bobby translated the situation for Gino.

Gino's mouth also fell open in synch with Pete's. "Angela?"

"Yes. Ange-fucking-la. Will you two clean out the earwax?"

Pete slammed his J&B and waved at the bartender for a refill. "But...why?"

"He wants me to teach her a lesson."

Angela DeMarco was Henry's third ex-wife. They'd married eight years ago when she was twenty. Their divorce was uglier than Pete's pockmarked ass—a metaphor that Bobby wished he didn't have in his head. Her lawyers couldn't touch Henry's money, since to the legit world, it didn't exist.

Angela knew it did.

She'd been making threats.

"What if she don't wanna be taught a lesson?"

Bobby threw back his fifth shot of Jack. "I kinda think that's the point, Pete."

Angela DeMarco's groans are muffled through the red rubber ball-gag as Bobby fucks her. The handcuffs on her feet and hands click on the frame rhythmically with every thrust. Bobby looks out the window and sees the Empire State Building gleaming over the river, like Manhattan's very own monstrous dick.

It's beautiful.

Angela screams. At least she tries to.

"You ain't gonna do it, are ya?" Pete asked as he rolled the handtruck into the back if the van.

"What choice do I have?" Bobby slid the jukebox off the cart and secured it in the hold, one of those new internet jukeboxes that all the bars in Manhattan had been switching to.

In with the old, out with the new.

Gone were the days when Bobby and the crew had to wrangle a half-ton of quarters into Brooklyn every week. These new babies took in mostly bills. Hell, they even took credit cards nowadays. In the last year, the new machines had tripled the cash money flowing into DeMarco Amusements.

Pete looked queasy. "We got enough shit to worry about right now, as is. Why the fuck is Henry even worrying about Angela? Christ, we got the Stella crew taking over the Meatpacking district, Chinatown's cut off, those crazy-ass Russians have all of Queens locked down now. I don't even want to talk about Koreatown. We're gonna have nothing left soon, and Henry's wasting our time with his marital problems?"

"That's Henry's choice, Pete." The real question that none of them asked was; why the fuck did Henry DeMarco do anything anymore? Why had he taken to wandering the neighborhood in his bathrobe? With all the money coming in, why hadn't he shored up his crew with more men than the current rotation of Bobby, Pete and Gino?

Their territory had been whittled down to Greenwich Village east of Seventh Avenue and was getting smaller every month.

If the Stella boys decided to take the rest of their territory away suddenly rather than chip away at it?

If they wound up in a sudden war?

Bobby knew that the pathetic DeMarco crew would be left, well…with their dicks hanging out.

"I don't want to sound paranoid, but…" Pete had been starting a lot of his sentences that way lately. The problem was, he didn't sound paranoid at all.

"But what?"

"When I went to clear out the machine down on Houston and Sullivan? I'm pretty sure I saw Chaz Stella's Caddy parked down the block."

Bobby stayed silent.

The two of them finished loading up the truck. Pete shuffled his feet as he unstrapped his back brace and tossed it into the cab. Bobby knew he had something on his mind when he did his little two-step, like a kid who had to pee.

Pete clapped his hands and rubbed them together. "Okay then. You doing the collections today or Gino?"

"I am."

"When are you going to do…it?" He wasn't asking about the collections any more.

"Tonight."

"Jeez." Pete looked like he might puke. Without another word, Pete clapped his hand onto Bobby's shoulder and grasped it tight.

They'd been through a lot together, done a lot of crazy, sick (mostly illegal) tasks for Henry DeMarco—but what Bobby was being ordered to do? That was something else.

Pete drove out the bay doors and went left on Metropolitan, heading for the bridge.

Bobby walked around the receiving desk, where Gino waved him over. Gino looked around the area, a little red-faced. He palmed something into Bobby's hand.

A foil wrapped condom.

"Per il tuo cazzo."

"Grazie."

When he finishes, Angela is slumped on the bed, her arms and legs dangling up like a marionette waiting for the show to begin. He dresses slowly in her bathroom, the bedroom silent but for Angela's strained breaths.

Bobby turns on the water and rubs his hands under the scalding stream. He slicks his hair back, not looking at himself in the mirror.

When he walks back into the bedroom, he gently uncuffs one of Angela's wrists, rubs the angry dark furrows where the metal dug into her skin and puts the key in her palm.

There's a chill in the night breeze and Bobby wishes he had a jacket. He climbs into his old Chevy and pulls onto the BQE, drives the two short exits to Henry's house.

The lights are on in the old duplex that Henry has lived in all his life. Bobby checks his watch—almost midnight. He presses the doorbell.

Henry opens the door in, what else, his bathrobe. As he looks at Bobby expectantly, Bobby takes a long look back at his old boss. The front of his dirty tee-shirt is covered in orange Cheez Doodle residue. The yellow powder is also clinging to Henry's unshaved lip and his hair is an unkempt mess. Henry DeMarco looks really, really old.

Bobby remembers the man he used to be. The dapper neighborhood wiseguy whose presence alone kept the whole block safe. The guy who always picked up the tab for his crew, be it at Burger King or Peter Luger's. The generous boss. The father figure.

But that guy isn't standing in front of Bobby any more. Not this batshit old psycho covered in Cheez Doodle powder who orders the rape of his ex-wife.

A flicker of a smile plays under Henry DeMarco's watery eyes. "It done?"

"Almost."

Bobby fires the gun into the old man's heart three times. He's dead before gravity catches hold of his lifeless body and drops him towards the floor.

Bobby catches him and lowers him slowly onto the worn hallway rug. Bobby kisses the old man on the forehead. "I'm sorry, Henry."

He gets back into his car and takes the long way back into Park Slope. Through some New York Miracle, he gets the same space he just vacated in front of Angela DeMarco's apartment. Two short honks and Angela comes running out the door, lugging her suitcase. "Pop the trunk."

Bobby shakes his head. "Trunk's full. Just throw it in the back seat." The trunk is filled with Bobby's luggage, ten grand in singles, and a hundred pounds of quarters from the jukeboxes. On top of all that lies the valise given to him from Chaz Stella with a hundred grand in it.

Angela opens the passenger side door and slides in. "Thanks for leaving me gagged and handcuffed, asshole."

Bobby shrugs. "Didn't want to hear you bitch about cuddling after sex again. You pack the handcuffs?"

"Nice. Real nice. Some gentleman you are. Good thing you got a big dick."

Yeah, Bobby thinks. *And if Henry knew that I've been sharing it with you for the last six months, it'd be me lying dead in a hallway somewhere.*

"Is it done?" she asks.

"Yeah." Bobby puts the car into drive and heads back to the highway. As Bobby drives by the Manhattan skyline, he looks over at the Empire State Building one last time.

Roses At His Feet

Jay-Jay rehearsed the lines in his head like an actor waiting to play his part. He'd close his eyes and imagine himself on a stage, audience applauding, spotlight bright in his face, roses tossed at his feet. In his mind, he was the playwright, director and actor of the two-man show that was about to unfold. Only the second actor didn't know he'd been cast yet.

It was art. He was a performer.

His venue; a tiny triangular park where Olive St. met Metropolitan, Orient Ave jutting it off at an angle. He waited on the dark side of the green, on Orient, around 3:30 each night and watched the bar crowd make their way home with a discerning eye. He'd watch for men with flowers, specifically.

Jay-Jay lit himself another Kool and watched the two young girls clinging dizzily to one another. They passed him without a glance, giggling at their own sloppiness as they zig-zagged down the sidewalk. Jay-Jay squeezed his crotch as they went. A tingle ran from the base of his scrotum and up his spine as he stared at their tight little asses shifting under the fabric of their tight little jeans.

He wasn't no mad dog. He had rules. First off, nobody drunk. Drunks were too unpredictable. Besides, most of them had spent their money on the goddamn booze that had gotten them there.

And drunks got ideas. Stupid ideas about their chances on the man with the knife.

Second rule, no women. Women tended to scream. Jay-Jay didn't need no attention.

It was all an art. It was all an act. Jay-Jay was an *artist*. He worked his fingers over the top of the chain-link fence, pretending the spaces were the ivory on the grand piano at The Blue Note. He played "Five Spot Blues", humming the notes as he jabbed at the imaginary keys. Shit, he'd been told a ton of times that he played it better than Thelonious Monk himself.

Crack or no crack, times were hard. Jazz clubs were shutting down left and right. Those few that were left had blacklisted Jay-Jay. Said the drugs were getting in the way. Making him fuck up.

Making him fuck up? Shit, somebody needed to tell those rich white motherfuckers who owned the clubs about *real* jazz.

Charlie Parker.

Chet Baker.

Billie Holiday.

Even Mr. Wonderful World himself Louis Armstrong smoked himself enough weed to choke out Snoop Dogg.

Drugs were making him fuck up? Fuck, drugs were as much a part of jazz as the goddamn instruments. Maybe more. Jay-Jay was waiting for the day that somebody, *any*body could explain Bobby McFerrin to him.

Jay-Jay started to work his fingers around "Cool Walk" when he saw him heading up Metropolitan. Not too big. Carrying roses. Not the pricey boxed ones, but not the shitty deli roses, neither. He didn't look drunk. Perfect.

Jay-Jay walked the opposite side, crossed over about twenty feet ahead of the guy. He kept the knife pressed against the leg away from the dude. No need to show his hand early. As he got close, he saw that the guy was Asian, wearing a green corduroy coat. He thought for a second that it was the same Asian guy he'd hit a month or so back. That cat had four hundred bucks on him. Jay-Jay was disappointed when he realized that it wasn't the same guy. Goddamn Asians all looked the same to him, anyway.

"Them's some nice flowers, my man." Jay-Jay smiled wide and friendly. The curtain was up.

"Thanks." The guy smiled warily, but kept moving. This was Brooklyn, after all.

"Psst." The guy turned towards Jay-Jay again. Jay-Jay flashed the blade under the streetlight. The guy tensed, but didn't flake—all good, so far. Jay-Jay motioned towards the flowers with the tip of the blade, liked the dramatic effect the streetlight (spotlight) had as it danced off the edge. "You got love, man. That's a beautiful thing."

The guy looked from the blade, to Jay-Jay, then back at the blade. Jay-Jay felt for a second that the guy still seemed strangely under-intimidated. He went on with his lines. "So I'm asking you not to risk that. All I want is the money in your wallet. You keep those flowers and you give them to your pretty lady. You hold her in your arms and you forget this happened. You don't, I cut you. I'm not playing."

The guy nodded, chewed on his gum, calm as a pond at dawn.

This wasn't right.

The five or six cats he'd pulled this hustle on shook a little, at least. One big guy started crying as he handed over his wallet. It didn't make Jay-Jay proud or happy to frighten those men, but it made him realize what a powerful tool their love was when turned against them.

Except with this guy.

Then he held out the roses to Jay-Jay. "Hold these a sec?" he asked as he reached behind into his rear left pocket.

Stunned, Jay-Jay took the roses. This guy was too cool. It was starting to freak him out a little.

He had his arms full of the flowers before it dawned on Jay-Jay that most men tended to carry their wallets in their right back pocket, not the left...

The flowers exploded silently up and out from Jay-Jay's grasp, red petals pluming into his face. He heard metal hitting concrete and saw his knife lying next to a hydrant. How the hell did that get there? Jay-Jay turned to see the Asian guy moving quickly, a flash of silvery light underneath the streetlamp and Jay-Jay's legs weren't under him anymore. He slumped to the sidewalk and leaned against the hydrant. Sticky warmth rushed down the arm that once held the knife. Jay-Jay went to grab it, but found he couldn't close his hand any more. Rose petals floated down around him, like fragrant crimson raindrops. Jay-Jay pressed his working hand against his side. More warmth ran between his fingers. Had this little chink fucker cut him? He barely even saw him move.

"It was poor form, Jay-Jay," the Asian man said.

"How...how you know my name?" Jay-Jay's lips were growing numb. It was getting harder to speak.

"I know who you are, because you made it my business." The guy crouched down next to Jay-Jay. He wiped his own wicked-looking blade clean on Jay-Jay's pants leg. "One of the men you robbed? His father is an important man whom I work for. Your robbery insulted them. They wanted me to find you, so I did."

Jay-Jay felt strangely calm despite the alarming rate that the warmth was escaping his body. The coldness in his legs was almost comforting, like a slow dip into the little plastic pool that his uncle would fill up on the hottest summer days.

Jay-Jay smiled a little at the flicker of memory from his Louisiana childhood.

He hadn't thought of home in a long, long time.

He looked into his slasher's eyes and was surprised to find them warm. "It was that Japanese kid I mugged, wasn't it?"

The Asian guy laughed as he lit two cigarettes with a wooden match struck off the sidewalk. "That's profiling,

30

Jay-Jay. So un-P.C." He stuck one filter between Jay-Jay's lips. "Besides, he was Chinese."

"Shit. I'm dyin', ain't I?"

"Yeah. You are. But you shouldn't be feeling any pain. I cut you cleanly."

"You're a fucking saint."

"I didn't have to." The guy stood. "It's a shame Jay-Jay. I saw you play at The Standard last spring. You were a great talent."

"Still am, for the next few minutes." Then he remembered his ruined right arm. "Shit, I'm not even that right now, am I?"

"Sorry."

"Tell me one thing…"

"What?"

"Did you think I was as good as The Monk?"

He shrugged. "I dunno. Never saw Monk play. But you can ask him yourself in a couple of minutes." Without a backwards glance, the guy walked back towards the L train.

Jay-Jay sat alone, his left hand tapping the bass notes of "Reflections" onto the concrete as he watched the rose petals floating by his feet into the gutter on a gentle river of his blood. He found it oddly beautiful as he died with a song in his ears.

The Long Count

'Ponk'

That was the sound in Rusty's head. Just like one of the cartoon sound effects on the Batman show. Unfortunately, it was also the sound of the big guy's pinky ring as it bounced off his upper left canine.

When the chirping birdies cleared, Rusty managed a response to the somewhat unexpected blow. "Ow."

The shot to the mouth was only somewhat unexpected since Hermes, the flyweight who had been working the heavy bag under Rusty's tutelage, took the first swing. Hermes was on his back, down for the long count.

"Aw hell," Rusty said, less in pain for his mouth than at seeing yet another prospect unconscious on the mat. Granted, Hermes was a flyweight and the puncher was clearly a heavyweight, but still. He should have been able to take one goddamn punch. Or had the reflexes to get the hell out of the way. "Look what you did to my boxer. That ain't right."

"Do I have your attention, Mr. Cobb?" The voice was a syrupy Texas drawl. Rusty leaned around the heavyweight to see its owner.

Jesus, Rusty thought, *I'm being rousted by Hopalong Cassidy.* The guy was standing in a Brooklyn gym wearing an embroidered western shirt and a brown ten-gallon hat. "Chaps."

"Excuse me?"

"You need chaps to finish that outfit, Pardner."

The cowboy nodded at the heavyweight, who grabbed Rusty by the front of his sweatshirt and backhanded him across the mouth. Small blessing, but the second shot cleanly knocked out the canine that was cracked by the first punch. At least he'd save on the dentist bill.

"Nobody likes a smart mouth, Mr. Cobb."

"Please, we've shared so much already, call me Rusty." He spat out his tooth, which bounced once and landed on Hermes's limp glove.

"This isn't a Sunday social, Mr. Cobb." The cowboy took his hat off and wiped his sweaty brow.

It was hot in the gym. Rusty kept it that way on purpose. A page he stole from the old Kronk Gym in Detroit for conditioning fighters. Maybe if he waited long enough, his two visitors would pass out from heat exhaustion. "So I shouldn't bother with the fine china, then. You mind telling me what this is about?"

"Don't insult me by pretending you don't know why I'm here." Cowboy bit the end off of a cigar the size of a biscuit can. He spit the wet tobacco right on Hermes's forehead. Hermes didn't even stir. One time contender, now human spittoon. The goon whipped out a lighter that looked like it cost more than a Cadillac. Cowboy puffed a few times, rolling the cigar for an even burn. "Don't insult me by telling me you don't know who I am."

Rusty tried. He didn't have to try hard. He was sure that he'd remember such a ridiculous character. Something about the goon itched at the back of his head, but that was it. As far as Cowboy was concerned, nothing. "Sorry, Hoss. Never really listened to The Village People."

Cowboy waved his hand wearily at Rusty. "Hurt him", he sighed.

The goon palmed the lighter like a roll of quarters and came forward for round three. Rusty was ready this time. It had been almost three decades since he'd been in a ring, but the moves were still there. Like riding a bicycle. A late middle-aged bicycle in desperate need of oiling, but still able to out-speed a heavyweight.

Rusty ducked the haymaker, crouching low and bringing his fist up and under the big guy's ribcage. The goon *woof*ed as Rusty drove his fist deep into his sternum. Then Rusty brought his left straight into the guy's balls. What the hell. They weren't in a ring, so Rusty wasn't worried about losing a point. The goon dropped to his knees.

God bless steel-toed boots, Rusty thought as he punted the goon's chin. The kick lifted him off the floor and on his back, splayed out next to Hermes. *Knockout*, Rusty thought proudly before he put weight on his kicking foot. Not being in fighting condition, the kick had wrenched his ankle. "Ah, shit," Rusty yelled as he dropped, clutching his foot.

Either way, he was just about to get up and hobble himself over for some cowboy ass-kicking when he heard the unmistakable click of a gun.

Jeez. The guy was actually carrying a six-shooter. Cowboy had it pointed directly between Rusty's eyes. "Nice moves for an old man, Mr. Cobb. I'd applaud, but I might accidentally pull the trigger and blow your face off."

"Please then, hold your applause until intermission."

"There is no intermission, Mr. Cobb. This is a one-act. At the end, you either return what you stole, or you disappear."

"Oh, it's like *Tony and Tina's Wedding*, then."

Cowboy didn't get that one. "You have three days." The big guy groaned and got up groggily. Cowboy shook his head disgustedly at his thug.

"That's a long play."

"You seem to be the only one playing here, Mr. Cobb. I'm not." Cowboy pushed the still staggering goon out the door.

*****

Rusty was a thief. A petty thief, at best. Stole petty items. Petty cash, for instance. Nothing worth the trouble that Cowboy seemed intent on causing him. No fine art. No heirlooms. Shit, more often than not, the jewelry that he pocketed fell into the categories of costume or out and out worthless.

Like a lot of serviceable but non-contender boxers, Rusty needed work not long into his thirties when it became obvious that his minor talents were heading south. He delivered packages for a messenger service. Sometimes, those packages were C.O.D. When the receptionist went into the little metal cash boxes, Rusty made mental notes. The next day, dressed in his only decent suit, Rusty would walk into the offices early while the cleaning crews were still working, stuff the box in his valise and walk right out. If he had to sign in at the security desk, he just wrote in S.R. Leonard. Rusty wondered if Sugar Ray had ever been questioned about the thefts.

His record low was $14.75 at a small dot-com. His record high was almost a grand out of some big entertainment manager. *Fuck 'em*, Rusty would think. He'd worked with a manager/agent for a few years. He even managed to get Rusty a cameo in a Chuck Norris flick. Granted, Rusty just got kicked in the head and played dead, but it was still pretty cool.

The sonofabitch dropped him faster than a handful of shit the second the ref counted to ten in Rusty's last fight. Rusty got a quiet enjoyment out of burglarizing those bloodsucking pricks.

If he came into an office that had expensive little laptop computers, Rusty would help himself to a few and pawn them for a couple extra hundred. It was that money that eventually enabled him to buy the old gym in Brooklyn. Nowadays, if he pulled a grab, it was more for shits and giggles than actual need. Some people liked blackjack for their gambling; Rusty enjoyed a little trespassing and B&E.

And it was all little. Little was the operative word. Worst came to worst, Rusty would only have to suffer minor legal consequences. Even when he hooked up with Dante, they made sure they took only cash and easily pawned items. For reasons he couldn't figure, Cowboy seemed to believe that he had something that belonged to him.

And he wanted it back.

Unfortunately, Rusty didn't have clue one what that item could be.

*****

"A cowboy?"

"A cowboy," Rusty sighed. Dante wasn't an idiot. He could sometimes be slow, or dull or…ah hell, who was he fooling? Dante was an idiot. But he was an idiot that could open safes faster than the people who knew the combinations. He was like Rain Man, if Rain Man had criminal intentions.

"Like Cowboys and Indians?" Dante asked.

"No, like Cowboys and Spaghetti-O's," Rusty yelled into the phone.

"Cowboys and Spaghetti-O's? I don't get you, Rusty."

Rusty shook the phone violently in his fingers, imagining Dante's thick idiot neck between said fingers. "Just listen to me, will you, dipshit? Has anyone been into the shop lately? Maybe wearing a cowboy hat? Walking his pet gorilla? Carrying a six-shooter and a lot of questions?"

"A gorilla?"

Rusty slammed the phone down. Dante was obviously off of Cowboy's radar. Dante had accompanied him on his last five jobs, going back three years. One morning, Rusty walked into an office and found Dante under the desk, looting a floor safe. He was dressed in a jumpsuit and looked as scared as Rusty felt. They stared at each other for a few seconds before Dante offered Rusty the glittering contents in his left hand.

"Halfsies?" he offered hopefully.

From that point on, they worked as a team. Rusty would scout the offices, determine which ones were worth hitting and bring in Dante for the safes. Dante brought his skills and Rusty brought his brains and helpful advice. Such as the suggestion that the retard didn't wear his A-1 Computer Service jumpsuit when he was going to rob a fricking office—the one with his goddamn name embroidered on the chest.

So Dante was out. Stupid, maybe, but Rusty doubted that he would just forget encountering the cowboy.

*****

Next step; information.

Information meant Jameel and the Candy Boys. The Candy Boys were a scam that ran its fingers through most of the city. A small army of kids roamed the streets, selling candy bars for their sports team at a buck a pop.

There was no sports team.

Jameel was the local sergeant for the Brooklyn troops. The kids got five dollars for each box they sold. Each box had forty candy bars in it. Buying gross, the boxes cost five dollars each. Thirty dollars profit on every box sold. There were more than a hundred kids selling box after box, 365 days a year. Nobody knew who was at the top of the heap, but whoever he was, he was one rich bastard.

Now the underbosses, like Jameel, ran a little side business. That business was information. Hundreds of eyes and ears across the city was an amazing resource. For the price.

"Two hundred."

"One hundred, just for the name." Rusty was uncomfortable standing on the open corner. Even though

Jameel probably had a couple thousand on his person at the time, Rusty wasn't worried about getting caught in the middle of a robbery. A while back, one of their sergeants got rolled. Less than twenty-four hours later, three teenagers were found under the bridge, throats cut, cheeks stuffed with M&M's. No, Rusty just worried what his neighbors might think.

"Don't have a name. Got something else. A hundred fifty for it." Jameel scratched at his belly. The front of his basketball jersey lifted, showing the hilt of a gravity knife in his waistband.

Rusty took the money and palmed it into Jameel's hand. Christ, he hoped nobody was watching.

Without even looking, Jameel rolled his fingers around the paper. "The top bill's fake."

"What?"

Lifting up the hundred to the sunlight, Jameel said, "See? No watermark. It's counterfeit, yo. You trying to play me Rusty?"

Rusty held it up, looked at it.

Shit.

He reached into his pocket and pulled out a crumpled wad of bills and handed them to Jameel.

"Only eighty-three here, Rusty. Falls a little short."

Rusty gritted his teeth. "That's all I have."

Jameel thought about it, then stuffed the money away. "Okay. The man's a Bleecker Street player. Don't know what his business is, but my boys see him at that blues club all the time."

"The Queen of Diamonds?"

"It's on the second floor, right? Above that Thai place with the big ugly ass orange awning?"

"Yeah."

"That's the one."

Rusty knew the club, but for the life of him still couldn't figure any connection. "How did he get pointed in my direction?"

Jameel chuckled. "Shit, man. How does anybody get information in this town?"

Rusty swallowed the hard lump that formed in his throat. "You told him."

Jameel grinned wide. "Damn right." Jameel could see the tension in Rusty as he clenched his fists. "What?" Jameel opened his arms wide, challenging. "You got a problem with that? The man had the cash and he paid. Not the bullshit scratch that you got, either."

Following his best survival instincts, Rusty turned and walked away fast, before he did something stupid.

"Nice doing business with you, Rusty," Jameel catcalled down the street.

Rusty wanted nothing more than to turn back and beat the snot out of the punk. He knew however, besides being suicidal, it just wouldn't look right, a grown man roughing up a twelve-year old like that.

*****

"Ah! My friend!" came the deeply accented bellow from the back of Abboud's Pawn. Rusty never liked the way Ali called him "friend". First off, he called everybody friend. Secondly, there was a slight undertone, as though he could replace it with "sucker" without missing a beat. "What do you bring for Ali today?"

"Just got a couple of questions, pal-o-mine." Rusty walked over to the plexiglass and chicken-wire cage that Ali cocooned himself in. For such good friends, Ali never even unlocked it so much as to shake Rusty's hand in twenty years.

"This no good information booth Rusty. Maybe you try Times Square." Ali hooted at his own joke. Rusty felt blood rush to his ears. "Maybe you go see *Rent*." Ali cackled harder. The only thing that ever emerged from Ali's box was his breath. The laughter pushed a wave over Rusty that smelled of yogurt and chickpeas.

"I'm serious Ali."

"So am I. *Rent* very good show. My children love it."

"I'm more interested in cowboys."

"Then see *Annie Get Your Gun*. Why do you bother Ali with no business? I'm busy man."

In those same twenty years, Rusty had rarely seen another human in the shop. More often than not, it was Ali's wife, who was usually screeching Arabic at him in a voice that reminded Rusty of a cat with Strep.

"I don't want to see a fucking musical, Ali. I got guys asking questions."

Ali's eyes made a quick flash from their usual greedy glow into fear. "What? What questions? What did you tell them? I run honest business."

"No you don't"

"Doesn't matter."

"Yes it does. They think I took something from them."

"What did you take?" Ali scratched his stubble, intrigued.

"I don't know."

"They no tell you?"

"They seem to think I should know."

"Ah! Is like movie *Marathon Man*. Great movie. 'Is it safe?' Did they ask you that? Did they ask you if it was safe?"

"Goddamn it!"

"Never mind. Okay, okay. What do you want to know from Ali?"

"Have I ever brought you anything…? Was there anything that you ever got from me that might have wound up worth more or wasn't what I thought it was?"

"No, Rusty. Ali would never cheat you like that."

Truth was, Ali would cheat anybody like that. But the reason that Rusty did business with Ali, apart from his moral ambiguity regarding purchase and resale of stolen goods, was that despite it all, he was a terrible liar. He was too greedy. Whenever he tried to pull a fast one or short-change, he would break out in a sweat faster than a pig in a sauna.

Ali wasn't sweating.

Rusty fingered the hundred dollar bill in his pocket. "I need a gun then."

Ali brightened back up. "Ah! Ali have many guns. Give old friend deep discount. How much?"

Rusty held up the hundred.

"Hundred is fake."

Rusty muttered a stream of curses as he stormed out the door.

Ali was still yelling as the door shut behind him. "Ali give you nice set of steak knives for bad bill! No gun, but you stab somebody good!"

Walking down Houston, Rusty turned into a quiet bar. He ordered a scotch, downed it, ordered another before the cute bartender put the bottle back. First luck he had all day. The bartender didn't catch the fake bill. God bless New York's bar scene, where perky tits outweighed brains and skill any day.

He sat in a cloud trying to think. Who was he kidding? He had nothing. He was five miles north of nothing and three west of clue one.

It couldn't have been anything that the cowboy wanted public, or else why not just send cops?

Weapons? By his best estimation, he'd acquired about a half dozen guns or so over the years. All of them went to Ali. Maybe one of them could have been evidence in a murder case? Nope. Figuring in the cowboy's style and readiness to draw, none of the guns he'd stolen were six-shooters.

Drugs? Nope. Couldn't have been. In many a safe, Rusty found the gamut from Valiums into what looked like a half-pound of uncut Colombian. They always left it behind. He and Dante agreed that drugs weren't any direction they wanted to head in, business-wise. Dante may have been an idiot, but he wasn't stupid.

Computers? Dante took care of the computers. He wiped out the hard drives, then sold them in his computer shop. Maybe there was some kind of damaging file on one of the computers. It still amazed Rusty that someone as mentally and physically clumsy as Dante could have such careful fingers on a keyboard.

Deft fingers that were capable of pocketing something before Rusty knew what was in the safe. Jumpsuits had lots of pockets.

Before Rusty could leap up and run over to strangle himself a retard, the bartender squealed and ran to the door. "Yancy! Get in here! You better not be walking by without saying hi." In the doorway, she leapt into a pair of arms, peppering the face with affectionate kisses. Very big arms. The cowboy's goon carried the girl back into the bar, placed her down and sat in the stool next to Rusty.

"Hiya Rusty," he said.

"Hiya Yancy. Funny coincidence isn't it?"

"What? Oh. Well, to be honest, yeah." Yancy actually blushed.

The bartender started pouring a pint before the tap sputtered and died. She clucked her tongue. "I got to go down and change the keg. Don't you leave." She pointed an admonishing finger at Yancy before she walked out back.

"Cute kid," said Rusty.

"Yeah. I used to work the door here. I was following you. The coincidence was that you came in here."

"This before or after Tua?"

Yancy looked surprised. "I guess it wouldn't have taken you long to figure it out at this point. Did you see it?"

"In person." Yancy Benevides was a young heavyweight who made the mistake of running into six too many of David Tua's hooks one night in Vegas. Rusty watched the whipping from the front. The fight was on the same card as one of Rusty's not-so-hopefuls. That was why he looked familiar. "Was that your last?"

Yancy tapped his right eyebrow. "They removed part of my ocular bone. Nicely dislocated my cornea too. Fucking Hawaiian hits harder than a mule kick."

"He's Samoan."

"Either way. Was Hearns your last?"

Now it was Rusty's turn to be surprised. "Yeah. The famous right. Did you see it?"

"Over and over. Broke my Dad's heart. You were his Great White Hope. In a way, I was kinda honored when you punched me in the gym. Until you hit me in the balls."

"Sorry." Rusty wasn't sure if he was apologizing for the low blow or for Mr. Benevides's broken heart.

Yancy shrugged. "S'okay, I guess. I'm gonna stop following you now, since you know I'm here and all."

"All right."

"Mr. Queen wanted me to tell you that you got one more day." Yancy caught himself. "Forget I said that." He tapped his eyebrow again as he stood in explanation of his gaffe.

"Already knew," Rusty lied. "Queen of Hearts. That where you met him?"

"Yup. Working the door."

"So, boxer, to bouncer, to goon? Dad must be proud."

Yancy shrugged. "Pays better than either of the first two. How much does thief pay?"

"Touché."

"Oh, and I owe you this." Yancy brought his huge fist down onto Rusty's crotch, mashing his testicles into the bar stool. Rusty moaned and slumped to the floor. When he found the strength to open his eyes, he was looking up at the bartender.

"You're gonna have to leave, Mister."

They are remarkably *perky tits*, Rusty thought as he wondered whether his balls would ever work again.

*****

The hole was small and right between Dante's eyebrows. Dante's vacant eyes were crossed, as if trying to look up and into the hole that had opened there. Rusty fought the crazy urge to look in the hole for any evidence of a brain. Instead, he rooted through the pockets of Dante's jumpsuit. Seventeen hundred dollars. Not bad. Rusty knew the old adage to be true. Nobody was more paranoid about theft than a thief. Lucky for him, Dante wasn't bright enough to find a hiding place anywhere but on his body.

It all came together in Rusty's mind. He'd been fighting the wrong fight all along. Never go toe-to-toe with a puncher when you're a boxer.

Last round.

Ding.

*****

Rusty left the message at The Queen of Hearts that he'd meet them there at five a.m. After closing, but before Bleecker Street would have any morning traffic. Rusty got off the train at Second Avenue and jogged the remaining mile, feeling his blood pump, the muscles loosen up. He felt good. He jogged up the stairs to the club, marveling at the god-awful orange awning as he passed it. He knocked on the wooden door. Yancy opened it and stepped aside.

Mr. Queen smiled a big Texas grin as he came in. "Mr. Cobb. I'm so glad that you decided to do business here, clean up the mess you made, and such."

Rusty pulled the metal box out of his backpack. "First of all, let me apologize for any inconvenience this has caused you. I didn't know what it was when I took it and I sure as hell didn't know how important it was when I did."

Queen smiled wider. "Bygones and such. Yancy?"

Yancy took the box from Rusty and with his other hand grabbed the hood of Rusty's sweatshirt, choking him.

Queen took the box and stepped back. "Just so's were sure you're not trying to pull a switcheroo here."

"Suit yourself," Rusty croaked.

Queen thumbed the lock on the box.

Three.

Queen opened the box. Rusty spun, catching Yancy with a hook right on the eyebrow he'd pointed to. Yancy let go of the hood and wobbled noticeably.

Two.

Queen looked up, his face a mask of rage. "You sonofa--" He dropped the box and reached for his gun. Rusty threw the dazed Yancy into the space between Queen and himself. Yancy stumbled and fell into the gun. His body muffled the shot, but a red blossom opened on his back.

One.

Rusty dove out the second story window into the ass-ugly orange awning.

BOOM

The explosion blew out all the windows facing Bleecker.

Rusty never figured out just what he was supposed to have stolen.

Dante's money had been enough to buy a timing cap and a small quantity of plastique from Ali. Small, but enough for one good bang. With ultimate caution, Rusty attached the cap to the lock on the box and stuffed the lower part of the tiered box with the explosive, turning the metal casing into a great big shrapnel grenade.

The concussion nearly threw Rusty over the awning, but he caught the edge, rolled, and came down hard on the street. He was covered with shards of glass, but the thick sweatsuit had protected him from any major cuts.

He lay on the concrete for as long as he could afford, did a quick mental inventory of his parts, decided they were intact and carefully got up. Time to go. His ears rang loudly and he feared he wouldn't hear approaching sirens.

On the corner of LaGuardia, Rusty found a slightly burned cowboy hat. He stuffed it into his backpack and started the jog back to Brooklyn.

Dirty Laundry

"How long has she been missing?"

"Two days," Nathan said, putting his Rolling Rock bottle on my desk. Condensation off the bottle dripped onto my desk calendar.

That annoyed me.

Everything Nathan Underwood did annoyed me. From his idiotic growth of hipster chin scrub down to the way he sat on the corner of my desk like he owned the place.

Not that I owned the place, either. The "office" for 4DC Security occupied the space beside the liquor room above The Cellar, Boston's favorite dank pit for cheap beer and God-awful garage bands. The only reason he was up there in the first place was because he was offering me money, which everybody knew he had. He hardly ever shut up about it.

The 'she' in question, was Nathan's girl, Matilda. We'd all heard of Matilda, but nobody had ever seen her. Considering how many nights Nathan spent at The Cellar, never with the girlfriend, led many to speculate that she didn't, in fact, exist. Some of that speculation also touched upon what kind of girl would date a blazing jackass like Nathan Underwood.

Millionaire or not.

Yet there he was, offering me money to find the girl who I had trouble believing existed in the first place. So much so that I had twenty riding on it with my partner.

47

Junior's bet was that she was real, but looked like the backside of a leprous rhinoceros

"Where do you think she ran off to?"

Nathan's good eye shot me a look. His glass eye stayed where it was. "I didn't say ran off, I said missing." The hard look didn't impress me. Nathan was taller than me by a good four inches, but softer than a marshmallow in the sun. He was more Goonie bird than goon.

"Okay, fine. Any ideas where I should start?"

"She said she was going to do the laundry. She never came back."

Then she must have had some clothes with her, I thought. Another indication that she just up and left the turkey, but I didn't say it.

"You got a picture?"

He placed a 5x7 on the desk. Matilda was a tall, thin girl, with reddish-brown hair and slate-blue eyes that looked through you, even in a photograph. The only thing that kept her from being stunning was the sadness behind the obviously forced smile.

"That a bruise under her right eye?"

"It's a shadow," he said, without looking back at the photo.

"Looks like a bruise." I did my best to hide the contempt I was starting to feel. Who was I kidding? I always had a shallowly buried contempt for him. His proximity just made it blossom.

"Hey, whose side are you on? She's missing. I'm paying you to find her. You want my money or not?"

"I'm not on any side. I'm not being paid to be on a side yet. You want me on yours? Drop some cash or get the fuck out of my office."

Nathan stood up and slapped an envelope on my calendar, next to the new water stain. "You find her, you call me. I'll double it."

I counted two grand. "I'll call you if I get anything."

48

I resisted the urge to slam the door off his ass as he exited.

Junior stood at the door of the bar checking I.D.s when I got downstairs. "What did Jerk-wood want?"

"He wants us to find his girlfriend."

"Hah! You owe me twenty!"

"Don't think so. She might exist, but she's actually pretty." I handed him the photograph.

He snatched the picture from me with the hand that had H-A-R-D tattooed across the knuckles. "I'll be the judge of...daaaaaamn."

"See?"

"Man, I wish I had that dickshit's money." Junior squinted and looked closer.

"No kidding, huh?"

"Hey, that a shiner?" He flicked a finger under his eye with his right hand, the one with C-O-R-E on the knuckles.

"Shadow."

Junior gave me his 'bullshitting a bullshitter' glare. "Shadow?"

"Yeah. I'll be back in a half-hour."

Fenway Laundry was full of Berklee students even on Thursday afternoon. I walked in and felt a dozen pairs of eyes on me. I knew some of the kids in there from the club and could feel a jolt at my presence, as if I might bounce them from the laundromat.

A young Chinese woman sat behind the register, scowling at a newspaper. She lifted her eyes long enough to sneer at me, then went back to the paper. Obviously, I represented some icon of bloated Americana to her. I would have to use all of the Malone charm.

"Excuse me--"

"Change machine over there," she said in a way that indicated that it might be one of her few phrases in

49

English. She pointed at the far corner with a long manicured nail.

"No, I--"

"Drop off over there." She pointed at the other corner filled with colorful laundry bags. Her eyes never lifted from the newspaper.

I held out Matilda's photograph. "Has this girl been in here lately?"

The woman slammed the paper down and unleashed a torrent of angry Chinese at me. Her finger whipped back and forth in the air, inches from my face. The words were alien, but the tone was unmistakable.

"Fine, fine...Jesus." I stepped back, feeling my ears redden. She was still yelling when I left. I've seen enough kung-fu movies to know that the word "gwilo" didn't indicate a fond warmth towards me. She said "gwilo" a lot.

In my hasty retreat, I plowed into a little guy carrying a laundry bag almost as big as he was. As we stumbled and flailed, I recognized the little guy as Nicky Bell, one of the local soundmen who sometimes worked the boards at The Cellar. Nicky skidded off the curb and dropped his laundry basket. I grabbed his frayed denim collar to keep him from toppling into traffic.

"What the frig, man?" Nicky grabbed my arm to steady himself, then saw who it was that nearly steamrolled him. "Hey Boo, you in a rush?"

"Yeah, escaping the Dragon Lady's fire breath."

Nicky chuckled. "Yeah, she's rough. You wash your clothes here? I thought you lived in Allston?"

"I do. Listen, you seen this girl in here recently?" I showed him the photo, hoping against hope.

"Matilda? Yeah. She was in here a couple of days ago."

My heart jumped. "You know her?"

"We've chit-chatted over the dryers, but yeah. You know she lived with that butthole Nathan? Dude with the glass eye?"

"He asked me to look for her."

Nicky's eyes went wide. "She's missing?"

"Maybe. Anything weird happen when she was here?"

Nicky frowned and shrugged. "Nothing that I could see."

Dead end. Dammit.

"Well, if you hear anything—if she comes in, call me at the bar?"

"Sure."

I looked back into the laundromat. Dragon Lady was still glaring at me through the glass.

I took my findings back to Junior. "I think she ran."

"Wouldn't you?"

Heavy footsteps sounded up the stairs. Somebody pounded hard on the office door. I swung the door open, ready to sock whoever it was. I found the angry red face of Nathan Underwood. I debated socking him anyway. "What the hell?"

"Look at this shit." He slammed a letter on the desk. On it was typewritten:

10,000 dollar or Matilda die.
Leave tomorrow
in laundry bag at Fenway
Cleaner drop off at 9p.m.

"Awww, hell no," said Junior.

I picked up the note by the edge. "Nathan, this is more than we agreed to. You need to go to the cops with this."

"No! No. Screw the cops and screw these guys. I want you to take this money and drop it off tomorrow." He dropped a bright blue laundry bag on the desk. The contents thumped.

"Is there ten grand in there?" Junior looked at the bag hungrily.

"Then I want you to follow the bag and take care of whoever did this."

I shook my head to clear out what I thought I was hearing. "Wait a minute. What do you think we're doing here?"

"You take care of them and get Matilda. Then you keep what's in the bag. Nobody fucks with me and my money."

I refrained from reminding him that his 'hard-earned' money came from the lawsuit when he was seven years old and lost an eye after he decided to play in an unguarded construction lot.

"Is there ten grand in there?" Junior asked again, hypnotized by the blue vinyl.

8:48 p.m. Junior and I sat in his '79 Buick that he, for one reason or another, had named Miss Kitty. We shivered in the late October chill, as Miss Kitty had decided to stop blowing heat sometime during Reagan's second term. October in Boston may not have been Minnesota bad, but it sure as hell wasn't Brazil either.

"It's Nicky," he said, blowing steam off his coffee.

"What are you talking about? Nicky couldn't kidnap a toddler without getting beat up. I'm telling you, Dragon Lady's involved. Chinese Mafia."

"Nicky said she 'lived' with Nathan. Why would he use past tense?"

"What are you, the Grammar Police?" I rubbed my hands together for warmth.

"Hey, your best proof is bad spelling in the note."

"Her English was about as good as your Chinese."

"How do you know Nicky's literate? He works with musicians."

"Good point."

"Besides, you're forgetting the Man Laws."

He had me there. It was damned good evidence. "Maybe…"

"Maybe nothing. What kinda guy has a full bag of laundry after he tells you he was at the laundromat two days earlier? What guy do you know does laundry every two days?"

"There might be some."

"When was the last time you did your laundry?"

I was silent. Junior and I often did the 'scratch and sniff' method of laundry assessment on our clothes. "September."

"First week?"

"Yeah."

"Exactly." Junior smugly lit a cigarette. I'm not sure how he pulled off the smugness, but he did.

I checked my watch. "It's almost nine. Pop the trunk." I climbed out the car and went around back. The trunk remained shut. "The trunk, Junior!"

Even from outside the car, I could hear him muttering. The trunk opened, and I pulled the bag out. Ten grand felt surprisingly light.

Junior rolled down his window. "Are we really going to beat on whoever walks out with that bag?"

"You suggested we go to the casino."

"Not the point. So we're basically going to be mugging the kidnapper?"

"That's one way to look at it. First and foremost, we're going to find Matilda."

"Then we mug the kidnapper."

"Then we take our fee. Functionally, this belongs to us now. How they want to give it to us is their business. You willing to get rough for your share?"

"For five grand, I'd step on *your* neck."

"That's comforting."

"Double or nothing says it's Nicky."

"Then I got twenty on The Dragon."

We shook on it and I walked into the Dragon's Lair. She was yelling shrilly at a trembling girl holding an armful of wet clothes. "No dryer in ten minutes. We close in hour!"

I tried my best to scurry past without catching her attention. One time, Junior and I fought off an entire biker gang by ourselves. They didn't rattle me half as much as the hundred-pound Asian woman. Scurrying, however, is best left to those under two hundred and thirty pounds.

"Hey," she yelled at my back.

I cringed and turned. She started yelling at me again. Why did this woman hate me so much? She used that "gwilo" word again. I pointed at the blue bag like I was returning something of hers that I'd stolen. I placed it gingerly on the drop-off pile and rushed out. I didn't feel safe until I closed the car door.

"It done?" Junior asked.

"Done," I sighed.

"Why are you sweating?"

We waited and watched the laundromat with all of the focus that two A.D.D.-addled morons could muster. At ten, the Dragon Lady locked the door and shut the lights.

No Nicky.

Nobody left with the blue bag.

Junior was jittery. "Man, it's freaking me out that there's ten grand sitting on that floor."

"Dragon Lady hasn't left yet." As I said it, she opened the door again and looked up and down the street. We huddled low in our seats. Even in the expanses of the big Buick, our combined quarter-ton of dude flesh was compressed uncomfortably by the huddling.

"You smell nice," I said.

"Touch me and die."

We watched her pull down the gate, then stroll down the street carrying the blue bag. "Ah-ha! You owe me forty now."

"If she brings that bag to Nicky, it's a draw."

Junior pulled out of the parking space and crept down the street at a respectable distance. We traveled ten feet before she stopped in front of a multi-dwelling brownstone.

"Junior! Follow her."

"What? Why me?"

"She knows me. She knows I'm looking for Matilda."

"Dammit."

He parked again and trotted over to the building as I crouched low. When she struggled with the door, Junior politely held it open for her. I saw him twitch as she for whatever reason rewarded his politeness with some of her venom. I swear I heard "gwilo" again. She walked in, Junior watching her through the door. Then he hopped back to the car on one foot.

"Why are you..? Where's your shoe?"

"Holding the door open. Move your ass."

We ran back to the building. Well, I ran. Junior bounded quickly. "Which apartment?"

"First floor. Last door on the left."

I knocked and covered the peephole with my palm.

"Who is it?" came the angry accented voice.

"U.P.S.," I said.

"No U.P.S. Go away."

Really? Who says No U.P.S.?

I held up three fingers. "On three?"

Junior raised his eyebrows happily and clapped his hands. "Breakie, breakie." Junior loves few things in this world more than wanton destruction.

"One-two-*three*!" We slammed our shoulders against the wood and broke through a little easier than we expected to. We tumbled through the shattered door into a thin hallway and landed in a heap on top of a very surprised Chinese woman.

If I thought I'd heard her curse before...

I grabbed an arm.

It was Junior's. "Agghhh! She got me!"

"I got you, Junior."

"No," he shrieked. *"She stabbed me in the fuckin' leg!"*

I turned my head far enough to see her pull a butterfly knife out of Junior's thigh. He screamed again and we managed to untangle ourselves in record time. We both had our backs to the door. Blood ran from between Junior's fingers where he had his hands pressed against his thigh.

She held the bloody knife at me menacingly. "You think you're tough, Underwood?"

What the..?

She thought I was Nathan. With an impressive flicking of her wrist, the butterfly knife danced around her fingers. Clearly, she knew what she was doing with it. "Want to try beating up on this girl?"

I held my hands up in a defensive pose. "Waitaminute! I'm not--"

Then Nicky came around behind her. "Boo? What's going on?"

"Boo? Who the hell is Boo?" asked the Dragon.

"Draw!" Junior yelled, excited that he didn't owe me another twenty.

Dragon Lady raised the knife threateningly, misunderstanding Junior's declaration. "You move your hands and I'll fillet you like a fucking chicken."

Then it dawned on me that her last two phrases were spoken in perfect English. "What happened to your accent?"

"Hey," Junior yelled. "Anybody care that I just got fuckin' stabbed?"

Matilda came up behind Nicky. She'd obviously taken a recent beating. Her lip was pooched out and swollen. A nice shiner rested under her left eye this time.

"That's it!" I hollered. "What the fuck is going on here?" Before anyone could answer me, something heavy hit the floor behind me. I turned to see that it was Junior lying crumpled on the deck.

I barely had time to react to my fallen buddy when the baseball bat came down onto my neck.

I must've gone out for a couple seconds, because when I opened my eyes, there was a chaos erupting in the living room that wasn't there the last time I blinked.

Nathan was standing in the middle of the room waving a baseball bat.

Matilda hung onto the arm wielding the bat.

Dragon Lady was on his back. I didn't know where her knife was.

Nicky was throwing pathetic kicks into Nathan's shins as he clutched his awkwardly bent arm.

Everybody was screaming.

Groggily, I stood, blood in my eyes. Nathan must have only glanced the shot off my head, since I was still breathing. Thank God for the legendary thickness of the Malone skull.

Junior was still unconscious on the floor.

Rage boiled in me as I looked at Underwood. The man who tried to knock my brains in. The man who might have just killed my best friend.

The room went red. Redder than the blood in my eyes.

I launched myself across the room and swung a straight right to his jaw with everything I had, plus another hundred pounds or so p.s.i. of pure pissed-off-edness. Considering the melee, I was lucky to connect at all. My fist cracked off Nathan's stupid fucking face with sufficient force to pop out his glass eye. Three bodies flew off the floor and landed painfully onto the hardwood.

The eye bounced off the wall and rolled to a stop between Dragon Lady's legs. Nathan was out.

"Jesus," said Dragon Lady. "You knocked his eye out."

We got this much sorted out before Nathan woke up.

Junior was fine. Well, as fine as a stabbed and bludgeoned man could be. Some cold water on his face brought him back. He barely had a lump on his thick head.

My head, however, was busted open behind the ear. I held a compress on it until I could get some stitches.

Dragon Lady's name was Cecilia. She and Matilda had forged a friendship in recent months over a shared history of pain.

Cecilia sat on an ottoman, holding a cup of hot tea. She stared into the swirling tendrils of steam as she spoke, like they were the rising ghosts of her past. "In Canton, my husband beat me daily. I saw Matilda coming in with her bruises and I had to ask."

"Is that why you're in the States?"

"That...and other things."

"Like what?" Junior asked suspiciously as he held a bloody rag to his thigh. The wound wasn't terribly deep, but he'd probably need stitches too.

"You don't want to know," she said with a wink.

Junior glared at her nervously.

"Why the fake accent?"

She shrugged. "Fewer people screw with you if they think you don't know the language."

I couldn't argue with that. "Where did you learn English?"

"*Buffy the Vampire Slayer* reruns"

Nicky had been a regular customer at the laundromat for years. A few months back, he'd asked Cecilia about Matilda. Cecilia could see his attraction and did her best to facilitate their romance. Their problem was two-fold (no pun intended). Nathan rarely let Matilda out of his sight for more than the amount of time it took to run errands.

"I couldn't get away from him," Matilda said softly. "He's crazy jealous. We couldn't go anywhere. I couldn't go anywhere with him. He'd always get into fights. He'd accuse me of one thing or another, then..." She bit her lower lip. "I knew he'd find me—that he'd send people to find me."

My ears went red. Junior and I had allowed ourselves to become Nathan Underwood's 'people'. The thought made me nauseous.

Their second problem was money.

"We couldn't run without any." Nicky's color was sickly pale as he hung on the arm that Nathan had broken with the bat. He'd have to visit the hospital too. Maybe we could carpool. "So we came up with the kidnapping. We figured Nathan wouldn't miss ten grand."

He wouldn't, but he did miss his house slave. Enough to try and kill us all. Luckily, he was as much a failure as a murderer as he was as a human being. "Where were you going to go?"

Matilda answered. "I have a brother in Detroit. We needed the money to get there." Water started welling in her eyes. The tear glistened on her shiner. "We were...I was desperate."

"Did you bring him here?" Cecilia pointed at the unconscious Nathan.

"No. He must have followed us."

"And you didn't notice?"

"Hey," said Junior. "You didn't notice us following you."

She narrowed her eyes at him. "I can find my knife, you know."

"Try it."

"I have others."

"Cut it out," I said.

"Muuuhhhhhh..." interjected Nathan. He tied to stand, but found it more than difficult, him being all tied up on the floor and all.

With clothesline rope, of course.

Then somebody knocked at the door.

Casually, Cecilia stuffed a sock (dirty, I hoped) into Nathan's mouth and slapped a strip of duct tape over his lips. He groaned a muffled protest.

"Who is it?" she screamed towards the door, the Dragon Lady back in the driver's seat.

"It's the Police, ma'am." We all froze and looked at one another. How the hell were going to explain this scene? "We've received a noise complaint." Cecilia was still cool as she walked down the hall. We all lay low and shut the fuck up.

I heard her swing the door violently open. "I watcha movie," she yelled in a tone that could shatter brick. "Why donchoo leave me alone?"

"I'm sorry, we--" The cop's authoritative tones immediately shifted into the defensive. Cecilia was goooooood at this shit.

"Why don't you go catch burglar?"

"I…"

"If I get rape, you gonna show up this fast?"

"No, ma'am…I mean yes, ma'am. Just please turn the volume--"

Then I heard the door slam shut. Cecilia walked back in the room and dusted off her hands. "See?"

"What are we going to do with him?" asked Nicky.

"Let's find out." I pulled the tape off roughly. I was happy to see a few hairs from his hipster scruff stuck on the glue. "Morning, Nathan," I said sunnily. "I wanted to thank you for popping me on the head with your bat. Now tell me why I shouldn't just dump you in the Charles River?"

Nathan gave a defiant one-eyed glare to the room. "I paid you, Malone. You were going to fuck me."

"I actually wasn't at that point, but I sure am now."

"I want my money back."

"You said we could keep it if we found Matilda. There she is." I gestured at the timid girl, making her flinch with just the hand motion. Christ, the poor thing was damaged.

Nathan sneered at her. She shrunk into herself under his glower. "You're part of this. I'm calling the police. Then we're going home. You're all going to jail," he said to the room at large.

Junior laughed.

Cecilia laughed.

I laughed.

Even Nicky laughed.

Matilda just sat there, staring down at her feet.

Cecilia placed a hand on her shoulder. "Say it to him."

She mumbled something.

"What? You got something to say?" Nathan's arrogance was remarkable, considering his position at the moment.

She held her head up sharply, a strength pulled across her features that I wasn't sure she was capable of. "I am not going home with you. Ever. Again."

This time, Nathan shrunk under her words.

She lifted her chin high, even as her jaw trembled. "I'm breaking up with you."

"Atta girl," said Cecilia, sounding more than a little like Sarah Michelle Gellar.

"Boo? Junior? Fifty thousand. Right now if you untie me and take care of these assholes."

Junior and I didn't move. If anything, Junior looked insulted, which impressed me. We had a price (and frankly, we came cheap), but only under the right circumstances. This was way beyond our circumstances. I knelt in front of Nathan. "Y'know, buddy? My mother got abused by a couple of her boyfriends. It's taking every fiber of my being not to stomp your head into tartar right now."

He started sweating when he saw in my eyes that I wasn't kidding.

I wasn't.

"Fine," he said and swallowed hard. "Jail it is, then." His voice was clear, but his eye was rapidly losing its bravado. "You're all going to jail."

"Ho-kay," said Cecilia, exasperated. "It's time we finished this, Canton-style." She walked into her kitchen. I heard silverware rattling.

The muscles in Nathan's face jiggled in fear. "Wh--what's Canton style?"

Cecilia re-entered with a mean looking butcher's knife in her fist. "You want to know why I had to leave China?"

Nathan started inhaling for what I could only assume was a great scream when I stuffed the sock back in.

"My husband used to beat me a lot, buddy. He broke my ribs twice." Cecilia undid Nathan's belt.

She couldn't be serious.

Could she?

She opened the button on his jeans. Nathan's eye bulged. "He knocked out all my front teeth. See?" She removed her upper and lower plates and wiggled them in front of Nathan's face. She put them back in her mouth and unzipped his pants. "I wanted kids. I really did. He beat me so hard I had three miscarriages." She roughly pulled his pants and underwear down. "I can't have kids now."

Then she grabbed his junk and squeezed hard. For a second, I thought Nathan's last remaining eyeball was going to come popping out.

Cecilia pressed her nose right up against Nathan's, fury ablaze on her face. "So I made sure he couldn't have any either."

She raised the knife.

Nathan made a lot of noise under the sock. I yanked it out. "Take the money! Take the money!"

"And Matilda?" I asked.

"Go! Go! God in heaven, please. I never want to see any of you again. Please just let me go." He was sobbing uncontrollably, snot and tears running down his cheeks.

"Too late." Cecilia drove the blade down with enough force to drive it into the floor two inches.

But about a half-inch from the ol' cock n' balls.

Nathan fainted dead away. His head made a pleasant thump as it hit the floor.

Cecilia stood and shook out a deep breath. With a wicked smile, she said, "Well, that was more fun than it deserved to be."

We split the money. Five grand each way was hopefully enough to cover our medical expenses and should have been enough for Nicky and Matilda to get to Michigan.

Junior and I dropped the unconscious Nathan by Fenway Park's C Gate minutes before the Sox game ended. We kept his eye. And his pants

Junior and I waited side by side into the emergency room. It wasn't the first time.

"You think he'll leave them be?" Junior asked as he flipped through an Us Weekly.

"I'll be shocked if he stays in Boston."

"Yeah. Wouldn't want Cecilia coming after me."

"Me either." Cecilia declined any money. Making Nathan cry was payment enough.

I looked at the lump on the back of Junior's head. "Doesn't look like he got you too hard."

"Nah. The puss swings a bat like a Yankee."

"Hard enough to knock you out a few minutes, though, didn't it?"

He didn't look at me. "I wonder if twenty-five hundred would be enough to hire the Dragon Lady for a freelance gig."

I shut it.

Last Call

I wait.

The bar is too clean, all pristine oak tables and shiny brass fixtures. The people are also too clean. The dudes all wear blue denim shirts with tan slacks. The chicks are decked-out uniformly in trendy black dresses and bottle-blonde hairdos like the girl on T.V. Hair By Stepford.

It's not easy being the pecan in the peanut gallery, surrounded by a hundred Brians. I miss the bars with the air so choked with cigarette smoke that the air hung in front of your face. They're all like this now. I've become less a man without a country than a drunk without a bar. This is not my New York. My New York is almost gone

The bartender checks my glass. I nod for another. She smiles, more for the tips than my charm. So far I've ordered four bourbons, but drank none. Despite self-awareness regarding my too-often consumption, not drinking is easier than you'd think. Without getting too Descartes-ian about it, I'm working. It's a personal job, but I'm still working. You fuck up in my vocation, the boss doesn't humiliate you in front of the cute secretary you're trying to bang. Nope. I fuck up and I spend a few decades in a concrete cage. Or in a box for eternity.

The barmaid leans over when she pours to give me a better view of her already ridiculously public boobs. It's her game, and it's not a bad one. I'm just not in a boob mood. Never thought I'd say that

"Love your shirt," she says.

She'll remember the shirt more than my face.

Friend of mine lives in the Upper West. Tells me he regularly sees this huge dude in the neighborhood—guy is like six-four, six-five—wearing a bright pink baseball cap. It's kinda weird, seeing this big guy in that hat. Fourth time my buddy sees the guy, he realizes that the guy is Liam Neeson.

Isn't that something? All that time, and all he saw was that pink fucking hat.

Liam Neeson is a man who knows how not to be seen. The devil is in the details.

I smile my best harmless, bland grin at the bartender. "Can't go wrong with hula girls on a shirt."

She giggles, takes the money and mouths a "thank you" at me with a sexy pout that probably made the frat boys drool in their Jager Bombs. I pour the liquor into the glass next to mine and sip my Coke. The night drags like church on Super Bowl Sunday. I wait some more.

I'd heard about Brian before I met him. Nothing good.

My day had already started out badly. My favorite watering hole, The Lady Luck Saloon, still had its metal shutters down when I arrived for my first libation of the day. I stood outside like a moron for fifteen minutes before I remembered that Andy, the owner, had "some bidness" to take care of in Jersey the night before.

Andy's known me since I was a kid, used to do gigs with my old man back in the days before the Alzheimer's took hold of my Pop. Most of the time, I do the freelance gigs today, family business and all, but sometimes Andy picks up a job or two here or there for some extra scratch.

I had to go with my Plan B bar and walked up to Dino's on 11th street. Dino's was a throwback bar, back to a time when keeping nodding junkies off the floor was considered hoity-toity on Avenue A. Most East Village bars nowadays seemed content working a faux blue-collar poser bullshit line. It isn't my scene; I hate Pabst Blue Ribbon and fedoras on wormy trust-fund babies.

Jeez, you'd think I didn't like pretty much anybody in the town any more.

I pretty much don't...

Josh, the bartender, jumped when the door banged shut behind me. He was chewing furiously on an unlit cigarette, looking like somebody had his nuts in a George Foreman grill. I glanced around. There was one couple sitting by the jukebox and a drunk old-timer swaying to the music over his beer. Unless Janelle, Josh's rumored pit-bull excuse for a wife was in the can, there was nothing that I could see that should have had the man so riled. Besides, Josh was six-two, sleeved in tattoos, and had been behind the sticks for twenty years. In almost any bar crisis, Josh was still the scariest man in the room.

Although I have heard that Janelle is scarier.

"What's got your panties twisted?" I asked, sitting in my regular seat in the far corner, facing the door.

"Hey, T.C. You seen Brian?"

"Brian who?" I helped myself to a bar napkin and daubed the sober-sweats off my brow.

"I don't know his last name. Black hair, always in a suit?"

"Not ringing a bell."

"Always makin' quick trips to the bathroom?" Josh raised his eyebrows and rubbed a finger under his nose in an unmistakable gesture.

"So what you're saying is, I don't want to know the guy."

"Probably don't." He took a deep breath.

"You know I don't."

Josh held his hands up, palms out. "Hey, I don't judge."

"Yes you do. That's precisely what you do."

"Whatever." Josh waved away my offense as he lit the cigarette and walked out the door for his tobacco constitutional.

Except the schmuck hadn't even poured me a goddamn drink yet.

I waited impatiently. In the meantime, I took another bar napkin and smoothed it out on the bar in front of me, hoping that when he returned he'd notice the conspicuous void on the mahogany.

Josh finally got back to his job, slightly more relaxed for the nicotine, and immediately tore back into the story. "So, this fucker, he was here all last night drinking heavy. Keeps making those trips to the bathroom and coming out fresh as a daisy." Josh popped another cigarette between his lips. If he stepped out for another smoke, I was going to knock him out and pour the whiskey myself.

"And?" I smoothed the napkin over with my fingers. Josh didn't notice. Not that I didn't want to hear his story, but c'mon. Priorities here.

"At closing time, either the blow was bad, or he'd hit the wall, but I gotta peel him off the bar." The wet filter between Josh's teeth split from his nervous gnawing. Josh made a face, pulling the white filaments off his tongue. "He comes back a couple hours ago in the same clothes as yesterday, coked off his nut again, just yelling and knocking over glasses. You believe that shit? On a fucking Sunday?"

I didn't know what it being Sunday had to do with anything in particular, but I said, "Go on..."

"I don't need this horseshit on a Sunday," he said, less to me than to the Vengeful Gods of All Things Bartending.

"What'd you do?"

"I go to grab him. You know what the sonofabitch does?"

I sighed, crumpled up my poor lonely bar napkin. Looked like my bad day had every intention of teetotalling my sad and dry spirit. "I do not."

"He pulls a knife. Says he's cutting anybody who touches him."

That made my ears prick up. In the years since New York went the way of the 1%, you don't hear so many stories take that kind of turn like they did daily in the bad old days.

For the record, to old-school cats like Josh and me, those were the good old days.

That said, I had an idea where the story was going. Josh keeps a Bernie Williams-Edition Louisville Slugger behind the bar for just such emergencies. "Will he live?"

Josh threw his hands up. "I didn't do nothing. He's an accountant for the fuckin' mob."

...uhhhhhh...

Okay, now.

And I'd thought I'd heard them all.

Every Bridge and Tunnel half-wit with a lick of Italian in his blood pulled that card at some point or another. Half the time, they weren't even Italian anymore. There's what's left of the Irish mob, the Chinatown Tongs and the Russians in Queens who were giving the Westies a run for the title of most psychotic crew in New York history. Hell, I'd even come across a few Japanese cats missing their pinkie fingers hovering around the karaoke bars in Little Korea.

Regardless, anybody who couldn't earn their own, said they're connected.

Or work for the mob.

Or grew up with yadda, yadda, blah-fucking-blah.

I knew the mob had better things to do than execute people over bar brawls.

First thing you learn out about mob and mob associates when you encounter a real one: Nobody claims to be mob or a mob associate.

Josh knew that too. He must have seen disappointment in my face. "I know, I know," he said, "but an accountant? Who the hell would say they're a mob accountant?"

He had me there. I'd have to wait for Andy to get back into town. He's better acquainted with those guys. I just freelance

Since it didn't look like I was going to get that drink, I decided to move on. Josh's nerves were interfering with my mojo. Besides, if Janelle walked in, the added stress might make his head explode, and I didn't need the dry cleaning bills.

I switched atmospheres and went over to Zen to see Vic and Bertie. Zen ran on the trendy rail, but the jukebox was decent and nobody bothered you with unwanted conversation. Bertie was five-feet-nothing of blue-haired smartass who drank too much while she bartended, but she reserved the only padded chair for me—in the far corner of course, facing the door. Vic was a soft-spoken monster of a man who watched over Bertie until the bouncer arrived.

Since she didn't charge me for every other drink and on my birthday she bought me a hula girl shirt, she was all right with me. Problem was, she liked causing trouble with her mouth. She often got herself into fixes and liked to see Vic get her out. She was just that kind of girl.

As I entered, Vic was talking to some guy dressed like he just finished shooting a Botany 500 ad.

Vic waved. "Hey T.C., come meet a friend of mine. Brian, T.C."

I'm not sure who I'd been picturing, but it sure as hell wasn't Johnnie Suburbia over there. How did I know it was the right Brian? He looked like an accountant of *some* kind, his pupils were the size of a ball-point tip, his suit looked like it had been slept in, and he worked his teeth back and forth like he was grinding corn meal in his cheeks.

Oh, and he had a line of blow trailing from his left nostril that almost touched his ear.

Looking at him, I realized that I could have sat next to him a dozen times and never remembered. He grinned at me like a man with a used Pinto to sell. "Hey Big Guy. Nice to meetcha."

I hate people who call me Big Guy. I scraped a smile across my face. "Hey." I tapped a finger to my nose. "Missed a spot."

"What? Aw, shit." He wiped his nose and cheek with the back of his arm. "Good looking out, brother. Whatcha drinkin'?"

"Makers." I glared at Vic. Vic wouldn't meet my eyes.

Brian waved at Bertie, who already knew what I was having and was setting it down on a napkin. She didn't look at me either. "On me, Bertie."

"Thanks," I said.

"No problemo." He threw the salesman grin again. He was quickly becoming the walking embodiment of my pet peeves. So far he hadn't smacked me on the shoulder or had his shirt label sticking out. Small favors. "So, what's T.C. stand for?"

"Thomas Jefferson."

"Huh?"

"My mother couldn't spell."

He didn't get it.

Brian leaned close, whispering, "You party?"

Ah. A peeve I'd forgotten. People who use "party" as a verb. "Define party."

He opened his palm under the bar to show me a small glass vial. I glared at Vic again. He looked over, winced when he saw what Brian was offering me, then put his eyes back on the bar.

"Not my kind of party," I said with as much friendliness as I could muster, which was none at all. Brian didn't seem to notice or, frankly, give a shit.

"No problemo." He laughed like a sick hyena and smacked my shoulder.

I downed my drink. "Sorry guys. Gotta run." I may be a drunken hypocrite, but I like to keep my vices safe and law-abiding, if possible. Just being next to the guy made all the old alarm bells ring.

As I walked behind them, I saw Brian's goddamn shirt tag sticking out.

Fifteen years ago, Vic and Bertie were young St. Marks squatters. So green to the Big Bad City, they smelled like the inside of a Greyhound. They quickly connected to the wrong scene. I don't know if they were shooting junk before they got to New York or if it got hold of them upon arrival, but they were fighters. I could see it in them the same way I see my own reflection in the morning, when the hangover is sumo-wrestling against my conscience. Only I don't fight it so much any more.

I watched them clean up, straighten out their shit, and build a semblance of a life together. Whenever possible, I'd slip them a few extra bucks without letting them know. I was proud of them. A lot of the St. Marks junkies from back in those days wound up doing the Sid Vicious bellyflop on abandoned tenement floors.

I wondered why Vic was hanging out with that jackass.

I hoped it wasn't what I thought.

After the unease of my sojourn into Zen, I made my way back downtown and finally caught a break in my shitty bar-hopping afternoon. I saw Andy opening Lady Luck's gate from two blocks north and had to restrain myself from breaking into a joyous sprint when I did.

"Don't tell me you've been waiting out here for me all day," he said as I approached.

71

"Might as well, the afternoon I've had."

Andy checked his watch. "Hmm. Three o'clock and you're stone sober."

We walked in together. Lady Luck was built around an old horseshoe bar, had about thirty pictures of Sinatra for decoration and high windows so that the cruel, cruel sunlight only trickled down into drunken eyes. All that, and Andy allowed me to pick the records for his jukebox. Only box in Manhattan with Big Mama Thornton, that I knew of. Best of all, Andy would break my arm if I ever tried to pay.

And I mean he would break my arm.

In many places.

But lovingly.

"How was Jersey?"

He shrugged. "Simple. You coulda done it."

"What's that mean?"

"I meant it was straightforward. Sheesh, you're sensitive when you're sober."

"What'd he do?"

"The guy?" He shrugged again. "He wasn't particular about who he stuck his dick into. Knew it too."

"Living dangerously, huh?"

Andy hit the light switches. "Used to."

My drink arrived before I noticed Andy making it. Everyone thought Andy was just a skilled bartender. That's not to say that he couldn't sling booze with the best, but I knew otherwise. Those hands had paid for the bar I was sitting at, and it wasn't simply due to his magnificent Mai-Tai recipe. He's sixty-six and faster than a man half that age. I know. I'm half that age. I've done the math.

I tasted my drink. "Andy, do you know any... accountants for the families and/or crews?"

Andy stopped counting the register bank. "Accountants?"

"Accountants."

He looked up and ran his fingers through his bone-white hair. "Never heard of any, but I'd have to assume they have some. Why?"

"Some cokehead's wandering around saying he is one."

"Probably just a jerk-off who says it to get out of jams," he said, dismissively waving his hand at the idea.

"Figured that, but why the hell would he claim to be an accountant? That's what I can't get."

"Good point." Andy cracked an Amstel bottle with his hands and sipped. It wasn't the screw-top kind. "Name?"

"Brian. Don't have a last name. Preppy-looking fella."

"He a problem?" Andy raised an eyebrow. I knew what the question within the question was.

"If he is what he says, he's certainly making a show of it. If he gets busted, well...he seemed soft."

Andy made a face like he'd just bitten into a cockroach. "I'll make some calls." In Andy's estimation, the worst a man could be was soft. Soft men would fold faster than Superman on laundry day to save their own asses. In our line of work, soft men could get you killed the same as a bullet.

My train of thought derails when the jackass claps me on the back, making my drink slop over. He laughs at a joke that I wasn't listening to. I resist punching his larynx and fake a laugh instead. He orders us another round, takes a gulp and staggers off to the jukebox. One more Dave Matthews song and I swear to God... While he's gone, I dump my shot into his glass again.

"You done?" The bartender asks, pointing at the wings I'd ordered.

"All yours." When the wings came out, I offered the jackass one, trying to at least appear friendly. He sucked off the meat and dropped the spit-covered bone on the other wings. I've spent the rest of the night fighting the urge to pull his scrotum over his forehead.

A few days ago, I walked back into Zen to check up on Vic and Bertie. Afraid of what I might find, I was a little ashamed at the relief I felt when I saw a new girl bartending.

I got a dirty look from her when I "ahem-ed" her eyes away from her iPhone. "Where's Vic and Bertie today?"

She looked up with an unusual amount of suspicion for somebody who doesn't know me. "You a friend?"

I got a chill at her tone. "Friend, customer. Take your pick."

"Then it'd be best if you talked to them." With that, her attention went back to the phone. Instinct told me Brian was involved. Couldn't tell you why. Instinct also told me it was already bad.

I spent the afternoon trying to find them at all the other watering holes. As the sun set, I ended up at Lady Luck again, confused and aggravated.

"What's wrong with you?" Andy asked. "You look like ten miles of cat shit."

"You seen Vic or Bertie?"

"Yeah, he came in looking for you. He seemed upset about something." Andy scratched his stubble. "Looked like he hadn't slept in a while. Circles under his eyes."

I wondered if his sleeplessness was chemically induced. "Did he leave a number?"

"Nope. Just asked if I'd seen you. I said, "nope". Then he left."

Damn.

Things got complicated fast. When a waitress from Zen came into Lady Luck, I got the first of several accounts about the previous night's hubbub. I asked who else had seen it. She gave me names and I tracked them down. In the end, I got five different versions from five different witnesses. It was like living in my own personal fucking *Rashomon*.

The story that I've accepted is the one I managed to piece together from the consistencies in each account. Brian was one of those consistencies.

No signs of Vic or Bertie. Amazing how you can see people nearly every day, spend hours together and never exchange numbers or addresses. I didn't even know their last names.

My patchwork story went as such: Closing time at Zen. Brian got rowdy. Rich, the manager on duty, told him to get the fuck out. Brian pulled his knife. Bingo, bango, bongo. Second verse, same as the first.

Rich claimed that Brian put the knife to his face. The waitress said he just pulled it. Then said she didn't see a knife. Then wouldn't talk about it. I guess she'd heard the same rumors about Brian's work associates and didn't want to be involved. One thing's certain. A knife got pulled. Threats were made.

At that point in the fairy tale, Mookie the bouncer stepped in. Mookie bounced Brian into the wall, then bounced him off the concrete.

Good bouncer.

I guess Mookie either didn't know or care about Brian's "connections". All accounts had Brian taking himself a decent ass-whupping. I smiled every time that part got mentioned. I wanted to buy Mookie a puppy.

For some reason, Bertie turned on Mookie and Rich, hollering at them. Bertie's got problems, but I couldn't understand her defending that chucklehead. Or didn't want to understand.

Rich fired her on the spot. Bertie went ballistic, throwing bottles and pint glasses at Rich and Mookie. Depending on whose story you believe, Mookie may or may not have shoved Bertie, then called her a name rhyming with "runt". It was possible.

Lord knows, Bertie could be a runt.

Bertie went home, and her version, whichever it was, got Vic stewing. That was when he came looking for me.

Maybe he wanted me to get Mookie with him. Maybe he wanted me to get Brian with him. Maybe he just needed somebody to talk to and cool him the fuck down. What I do know is that he wasn't looking to employ my services. Apart from Andy, almost nobody knows what I really do.

Three days passed. I kept missing Vic and Bertie. The few people that ran across them all agreed that they looked...wrong.

I started to wonder if I was being avoided. If somebody wants me, I'm easily found. By the same token, if somebody wants to avoid me, they know where I won't be.

I kept looking out, but shit, I wasn't going to kick doors in for them. They were good people, people I considered friends in a life where I didn't have many, but they were adults. If they'd made some stupid-ass decisions over the last couple weeks and were tumbling back down the rabbit hole again, it wasn't my responsibility to throw them a line to climb back up.

It made me sad to think about it, but like I said, they were fucking adults.

So for the most part, I tried not to think about it.

Then Mookie was dead.

Just when I thought that the situation had run out of both shit and fans.

All I wanted was the goddamn weather on channel 4, and I got a motherloving murder. I almost choked on my bagel, coughing a mouthful of cream cheese and coffee right into the pretty newscaster's face on my tee-vee.

Bad way to start a morning, let me tell ya...

Some kids playing in a garage found Mookie next to his car. He'd had the unholy shit beaten out of him. He wasn't D.O.A., but he was D.S.A.

Dead Soon After.

The cops said a skull fracture killed him. They had no suspects.

But I did.

Brian suddenly jumped from minor irritation to legit problem. I didn't know who he did the books for, but I could only assume he was doing a bang-up job if they were willing to throw a hit his way. Hits aren't cheap, or given casually.

If it *was* a hit, it was the most trivial thing that I'd ever heard a hit put out for, and believe you me, I've seen a lot of people die over trivia.

Like I said—*if.*

I couldn't imagine Brian getting his own hands dirty, though. He was too fond of talking big and making threats. No real violence had happened around him.

Yet.

I hauled over to Lady Luck to see if Andy had anything. Like me, Andy was a creature of habit. He'd be there before opening, drinking espresso and reading the paper with his daily bran muffin. He hated the muffins, but at his age, he considered them half-breakfast, half-medicinal.

I needed some hair of the dog. Shit, I needed the whole Westminster Dog Show the way I felt.

I knocked on the door. Andy unlocked the bolt then sat back down at the bar where the crossword and his accursed bran muffin waited.

I locked the door behind me. The weight of the room hit me like an open-handed slap as I entered.

I smelled menthol cigarettes. Andy doesn't smoke anymore, much less menthols. He glanced at me and then towards the back. Vic sat alone in a booth.

"Been waiting for you," Andy said. "You know where the Makers is."

I helped myself to a couple of fingers, belted it and refilled before I went over to Vic. I slid into the opposite bench, smelling days worth of scotch seeping off of him. Vic looked tired, his clothes wrinkled and dirty. His fingers trembled on the cigarette, ash spattered the table. I didn't say a word. He was the one who needed to talk, came looking for me.

We drank in funereal silence. Every time Vic tried to talk or even look at me, tears would well and the silence would stand. I didn't feel it was my place to ask the questions.

Instead, we just sat and quietly drank the city away. An hour passed. Vic had four more drinks, slipping deeper into himself with each sip.

Then on unsteady legs, Vic stood up and leaned into my ear. He whispered, "I didn't mean it."

Without looking up, I heard him stumbling out the door.

The room remained quiet for a few seconds after he left.

"They're using again," Andy said into the newspaper.

"How do you know?" It was a stupid question. Andy would know. I knew. I just wanted to ask, to carve the slightest sliver of doubt off of the truths that I was ignoring.

"Vic shook my hand. Saw tracks on his wrist. If he's that far down..." He knew that I could finish the sentence without him having to. "She was here earlier. Kept scratching her forearms. Long sleeve shirt seem right to you on a day like today?" The newspaper rustled.

I swallowed my anger. "The accountant?" The words were acid in my mouth.

"Him?" Andy licked his finger, turned the page of his Post. "Used to work for the Dohnaghy's up in Yonkers." Andy lingered over "used to". "Full name's Brian King. Mickey Dohnaghy seems to think the kid's a prick."

That was all I needed to hear.

They buried Mookie. Brian disappeared. I didn't waste my energy looking for him. I figured he would rear his head eventually. At which time, I would eagerly express my disapproval.

Only all hell broke loose first.

When I showed up at Dino's yesterday, the joint looked like Detroit after the riots. Angie, the owner, stood behind the bar with a stunned expression, looking over the wreckage of her bar. The air was tangy from the bleach that the Mexican kids were slathering over the floor. Even under the bleach, I thought I could still smell...

...blood?

"What the hell happened here?" I said. "Where's my stool?"

"Vic and Bertie..." She opened her mouth twice to continue, then completely lost her shit, collapsing into sobs. It took a lot of comforting and even more tequila to stifle her tears and get to the goddamn story.

Vic and Bertie were at Dino's the night before. Somebody walked in and blasted Vic with a shotgun.

Just like that.

He was probably dead before he hit the ground. I hope he was.

Two pieces of buckshot caught Bertie in the throat. She took a while. Bertie lay on the bar floor, bleeding out while the ambulance took its time.

You know that a pizza will get to you faster in Manhattan than an ambulance? Been proven. Look it up.

By the time paramedics arrived, the only person alive in the bar was Josh, who'd caught some glass in his face. He tried to stop Bertie's bleeding using his shirt without strangling her. It didn't matter. He'd have been better off ordering a fucking pepperoni pie and hoping the delivery kid had CPR training.

Vic was in my barstool when the shotgun vaporized his chest, taking my stool with him.

Josh only caught a glimpse of the shooters. They were in ski masks.

The tally: Three people and the barstool that I'd spent years molding to my ass were dead. All tracing back to Brian, a big mouth who backed it up with a little knife.

He wasn't hard to track. His mouth cut a path like the runway lights at LaGuardia. Even in bars where his name wasn't known, his behavior was. He'd been kicked out of a few places and pulled his knife at one. The path led uptown. I followed.

As I moved north, I'd catch news reports. Even in a city as violent as New York, the Dino's Massacre (as it was called) was a sensational story. The media ate it up. The cops moved fast. Within hours, a shotgun was found in the trunk of a Chevy, the same Chevy witnesses saw burning tracks away from Dino's. By nightfall, the cops had Mookie's brothers in custody.

Somewhere in my shallowest sense of self, I felt sorry for them. Amateurs.

So I wait. He gave me a look when I walked in, but without recognition. I bought him a round and fed him my shots. He almost got into a fight with a kid at the pool table. He reached into his pocket and I reached into mine. His knife didn't come out, so neither did my .45. That's okay. He'll pull it eventually. He always does. Everyone will see who pulled first.

I'll wait.

And all I'll leave behind is the memory of an ugly shirt.

Hot Enough For Ya?

Jimmy Romance felt the blood drain from his face like somebody pulled out the stop plug in his neck.

"So joo had no idea that she was his daughter?" asked Ricardo with a smile as he leaned on the countertop of Jimmy's Tan-O-Rama. He asked the question slowly, savoring the words like a fine wine.

Jimmy couldn't answer the obvious question since his mind was still spinning with the new information.

The girl with whom he'd recently broken several laws of New York State, physics, and nature with, was the one and only daughter of the one and only Jonathan Bass.

Or, depending on who you asked, "Butcher" Bass.

And asked quietly.

Jimmy thought he might vomit right into his brand new tanning bed.

Ricardo clicked his tongue. "Of course joo didn't know. Because…"

Jimmy didn't need Ricardo to finish. The rest of the sentence would have been something about sado-masochism, death wishes, or both. "Does he know yet?" Jimmy hated the tremble he heard in his voice.

"Oh, he knows," Ricardo said, grinning, his gold incisor winking at Jimmy. Ricardo was the type of guy who liked to bring sour grapes to the dinner table. The kind of guy who only talked about the movies he didn't like. The restaurants with sucky food. The bad luck around the neighborhood. And he did it with glee. Ricardo was a ghoul for the jinxed residents of the West Village. "She come home last night wearing somebody's old bowling shirt. The one with Jimmy R. embroidered over the pocket?" Ricardo traced a finger over his heart.

Jimmy felt another wave of nausea run roughshod through his intestines. "How do you know this?"

"I heard Jonathan hollering as I passed by getting the paper this mornin'. Sounded kinda juicy, no offence, so I hung around front to hear."

That alone didn't bode well. Jimmy knew that Bass's apartment occupied the top floor of a brownstone on Thompson Street. If Ricardo heard him from the sidewalk, then he was yelling pretty fucking loud. What little Jimmy knew about Bass included his soft-spoken demeanor.

And that he preferred to do his loud talking with very sharp pieces of metal.

Wait a minute here. "Home? She still lives at home?"

"She only sixteen, Jimmy."

That did it. Jimmy ran into the can and lost his breakfast burrito into the toilet. "Ohgodohgodohgod", he muttered to the soon-to-be dead man in the mirror.

How? HOW the fuck could she be sixteen? She took it in the ass! Sixteen-year-olds didn't take it in the ass.

Did they?

Oh sweet fucking God…

He'd stuck his dick into the underaged anus of Butcher Bass's daughter.

Ricardo rapped 'shave and a haircut' on the bathroom door. The blood flooded back into Jimmy's brain with a roar. Was that little prick making some kind of joke? They both knew the rumors about Butcher's weapon of choice; a straight razor. "Hey Jimmy? Joo okay in there?"

Jimmy burst out of the bathroom and grabbed Ricardo by the neck, slamming him back into the counter. "Why are you telling me this! What's your play here, fucko?" he screamed, spittle flying in Ricardo's face. Jimmy knew Ricardo had a play, Ricardo always had a fucking play.

Ricardo only smiled condescendingly into Jimmy's outburst. "Cuz I'm a friend, Jimmy. I figure maybe somebody should keep an eye on the salon while joo away."

Away.

That was it all along. Ricardo knew that he'd need to go away. Where the hell was he supposed to go? Didn't matter. They could sure as hell find him here.

Mean Gene popped into Jimmy's mind's eye. Bass's cause and effect man. As in, cause Bass any grief, Mean Gene Ricciardi effects serious damage on your ass. Then he brought you to The Butcher for the big finish. Mean Gene had just been here a couple of months ago before his vacation.

Where was he going?

Paris. That was it. He said he wanted to get a head start on his tan. Jimmy remembered thinking of that crap movie, An American Werewolf in Paris. Gene could have passed for one if he had twenty percent less body hair and better people skills. Jimmy spent an extra hour Windex-ing Mean Gene's black curlies off the tanning bed.

Man oh man. Jimmy was woozy with the realization of just how big a world of shit he was suddenly in.

He had to go.

Fast.

"How much you got?" he asked Ricardo.

"Well, I got a couple hundred on me that I can give joo until..."

Jimmy caught Ricardo with a hard uppercut to the chin. Ricardo's jaw snapped shut with a sound like cracking ice. He stumbled, leaning backwards into one of the empty tanning beds. Jimmy slammed the top of the bed shut with all his weight on top, sandwiching Ricardo's face in the bed. Something crunched in the machine and

Ricardo slumped to the floor, blood pouring from his ruined mouth and trickling from one ear.

Jimmy felt Ricardo's neck. He still had a pulse. Good for him.

He reached into Ricardo's pockets, took the money and dropped the keys to the salon on the floor. He wouldn't need them because he wasn't coming back.

Couldn't come back.

Ever.

Jimmy noticed the gold incisor catching the light again. Unfortunately for Ricardo, it was on the floor, next to his right foot. Jimmy picked up the tooth and stuck it in his pocket.

"Hi," he'd said. Like most of life's grandest clusterfucks, this one had started out simply enough. Jimmy could tell with just that one little word whether or not to continue talking to the girl two seats over or to flash his practiced fuck-me smile at another. And there was always another.

Jimmy thought she looked young, but fuck it, they were in a bar. How young could she be? The big goon in the Jets jersey sitting at the door must have carded her on the way in.

She was decked out in a black leather miniskirt and a gold spaghetti-strap tank that showed off her flat belly and clung to her nipples nicely. She was obviously looking for some attention. The only kind of attention that Jimmy gave women.

"Mm-hey," she replied through her ruby-lipsticked mouth, a small daub of crimson makeup smeared under her plump lower lip.

Jimmy gauged the situation so far as very good. Her eyes had the soft glaze that indicated she was just past her alcohol tolerance. In the twenty minutes he'd been sitting there, she'd popped back two and a half apple martinis. *A little more grease*, Jimmy thought, *and this engine is a-runnin'*.

"Want to do a shot with me?" he asked. "I hate dinking alone."

The rest, until that cocksucker Ricardo came strutting through the door, went exactly as planned.

Jimmy made a mental note to stab that fucking bouncer in the throat if he ever saw him again.

The paranoia was the worst part. It had been five days since Jimmy ran from the Tan-O-Rama, hauled his ass to 14th Street, dove into a cab and got home to Brooklyn. He hadn't opened his door since.

Although Jimmy would be willing to bet that most people he'd known for a decade or more didn't even know real last name, he wasn't taking any chances.

Everybody called him Jimmy Romance.

Romance wasn't his real last name, of course.

Jimmy earned the moniker from the long trail of women that he'd conquered over the years. They were his Achilles Heel. His one weakness. Jimmy didn't smoke, didn't drink to excess, didn't do drugs. Clean as a bean. It wasn't out of any moral or health concerns that he'd kept himself so straight-edged, it was the pussy. Didn't smoke, because he liked to keep his breath clean and teeth polished, was often complimented on his pearlies. Drugs and alcohol killed his game, fucked with the brain and body. His mind was his greatest seductive tool. His body closed the deal. Why waste the money anyway? The intoxicant under the panty line was Jimmy's only drug. It was all he wanted.

The irony wasn't lost on Jimmy.

It was women that kept him in prime physical condition over the years.

It was one girl that might end up killing him.

He didn't know if anybody knew where he lived, but was pretty certain nobody did. Was his address written down anywhere in the salon? He couldn't remember for sure. It must have been. Was it anyplace obvious? Jimmy could just imagine that grinning prick Ricardo handing his address over to The Butcher for his thirty pieces of silver. Not having as much as looked at a Bible since Sunday school, Jimmy didn't recall Jesus busting Judas's teeth onto the floor before the betrayal, but wouldn't have thought any less of Jesus for it.

Nor did Jimmy plan on going peacefully into his personal crucifixion. During the few short hours that he slept, when he felt his eyes going too heavy for even the terror to keep open anymore, he would slide his recliner to the end of the long hallway and drift into an uneasy sleep, revolver in hand. On two separate occasions, he'd almost shot a Jehovah's Witness and a Girl Scout when they woke him up in a frenzied panic out of his tortured dreams.

Dreams about sharp things. Lots and lots of sharp things.

Jimmy wondered how much longer he could keep it up.

Pun definitely not fucking intended...

He was running out of food, for starters. His last meal consisted of oily old sardines on chewy rye crisps. He couldn't remember buying the dusty can of sardines. Who the hell bought sardines? Either way, in the moment, Jimmy was glad he had them.

He lived in New York, for chrissakes, where anything at any time could be delivered to your doorstep, but Jimmy was afraid to get anything brought to his house. He didn't need anyone to know that he was home. He would carefully watch the street from behind the thick curtains for any unusual cars, but what qualified as an unusual car? Jimmy didn't know his neighbors, much less what they drove on a regular basis.

The dark van with tinted windows, for instance. There was a dark blue Caravan that sat kitty-corner to his front window and didn't move for three days. Then on Saturday, some loser in full clown get-up filled the back of it with bright balloons. How the fuck could Jimmy live next to a clown and not know? For some reason, he felt he should have possessed that little nugget before this point.

On the fifth afternoon, as Jimmy prepared himself a lunch of watery clam chowder (he'd run out of milk) and a Froot Roll Up, he heard footsteps on the porch. Jimmy pulled the gun from his waistband, and pointed it down the hallway. It was just about time for the mailman, but Jimmy wasn't going to be taking any chances. The footsteps were heavy. Whoever it was, they weren't feeling any need for caution.

A sharp squeak. Jimmy cocked his gun with a shaking thumb. Rustling papers and the click of the door slot snapping shut. Without thinking about it, Jimmy hadn't even checked his mail for the four days he'd kept himself a prisoner inside the apartment. Too close to the windows. Also, somewhere in the back of his mind, he feared a letter bomb, even though it wasn't even close to Butcher's style. The Butcher liked cutting people, if that could be thought of as a style. John Bass liked his punishments delivered first hand and close up. For hours and hours at a time.

Jimmy crept carefully over to the door and collected the pile of mail off of his doormat. It was the typical mélange of crap. Gas bill, phone bill, some toolbag pleading for his City Council vote, credit card applications...

...wait a minute.

There it was.

He didn't know how long it had been there, but right there, printed gaily on a five-by-seven postcard was his salvation.

"Fortune Estates," came the sugary voice on the phone.

"...."

"Excuse me?"

Jimmy cleared his throat, realized that he didn't need to whisper "Yeah, I got your postcard."

"Excellent! So, as I'm sure you can see from the pictures that Fortune Estates offers the highest in quality living arrangements in t--"

"I want to see it."

"What? Oh, um...okay." The girl obviously wasn't accustomed to such an easy sale. "I'll need to check your name in our database. When would you like to see--?"

"Soon as possible. Name's James Romancelli."

"Well, Mr. Romancelli, I can send you the information packet in a week and..."

"I only have the next few days off. I can fly in the next two days or I can't fly out at all. You can overnight the ticket."

"Oh. Okay. Well, I'll need to check with my manager and see if that's possible."

Jimmy was put on hold to the strains of muzak Rod Stewart. He hated the real Rod Stewart. What the fuck made these people think that anybody wanted to listen to the muzak version? Jimmy's foot tapped on the floor anxiously.

The line clicked back. "Mr. Romancelli?"

"Yeah."

"I've brought your situation to the attention of my supervisor, Mr. Casey, and he said that we can help you."

Jimmy exhaled the breath he didn't know he was holding in and almost broke into tears of relief. "That's great."

"I'll send your ticket tonight and we'll see you on Wednesday. Is there anything else..?"

Jimmy hung up the phone and sagged against the wall. He had his out. His ticket, literally, would be in his hand the next day. Up to that point, Jimmy's running potential had been limited. With the money he'd taken from the register and out of Ricardo's pockets, he'd amassed a sum total of $1,022.36. Not nearly enough to run—and run as far as he felt he needed to in order to be safe. Not enough to start over. He had a couple grand more in the bank (and

Ricardo's tooth), but couldn't access it, not wanting to go out in public and such. But now, he got himself a free ticket to another time zone. He could get his money and live for a couple months while he set himself up. The operating words being he could live.

All he had to do was take a look at some dinky little timeshare. The location was the icing on his getaway cake.

Jimmy Romance was going to Vegas, baby.

Strutting through McCarran airport, Jimmy heard Dean Martin singing "Ain't That a Kick in the Head?" on a loop through his brain.

How lucky can one guy be?

You better believe Jimmy felt lucky. And what better city to be lucky in? He felt like a million bucks. He felt better than he had in years. He felt...free. He walked with a Rat Pack bounce through the terminal, all the way to the goofball holding a handwritten sign that read 'Fortune Estates' and 'Romancelli' underneath.

Check this guy, Jimmy thought. Only somebody truly living the good life could afford to dress so stupid. First off, the guy was wearing a white linen suit that looked like he'd bought it for a nickel at Don Johnson's yard sale. His peroxide-blonde coif was moussed tighter than a Catholic girl's bra strap.

Actually, as Jimmy looked around, he was a little startled to see how much color everyone wore. Jimmy was the only person in the terminal wearing full black. New Yorkers stuck to their black clothes like they were participating in a seven million-man wake. The wardrobe that would have blended him seamlessly into the teeming masses of Manhattan made him stick out in Vegas. Jimmy suddenly felt obvious and uncomfortable.

The guy caught Jimmy's eye. "Mr. Romancelli?"

"Call me Jimmy."

The guy smiled with teeth even whiter than Jimmy's, whiter than nature ever intended. Apart from the guy's skin, which was tanned a George Hamilton brown, everything else looked bleached to the bone. Jimmy shook his hand and smiled back, trying to make it look friendly, rather than the mockingly superior East Coast smile he felt worming onto his lips.

"Norman Casey, sales manager for Fortune Estates. But please, call me Norm." Norm extended a pristinely manicured hand at Jimmy.

Jimmy, took it in his own, suddenly feeling self-conscious for the first time in his life about the state of his cuticles. "You got it, Norm. So, what's the deal?"

"Well, first we'll get your luggage. Then I'll drop you at the hotel. No hard sell tonight. Tonight, you get to enjoy Sin City at your leisure."

"Sounds good, Norm."

"You expecting someone?"

"Huh?" Until Norm pointed it out, Jimmy wasn't even aware that he'd been nervously glancing from person to person around the terminal. The fear had crept back into Jimmy's subconscious when he realized that his outfit made him noticeable; a target if someone was looking.

Jimmy didn't appreciate the fear returning and did his best to push it back. "Nah. just taking it all in, Norm."

"First time in Vegas?"

"First time out of New York State."

"Well, you picked a hell of a time to see the desert, my friend.

When the automatic doors whooshed open, the heat nearly knocked the breath out of Jimmy. "Jesus."

"Hot enough for ya?" Norm cackled.

Jimmy couldn't believe that he actually asked that. "This whole place is like a big fucking Tandoori oven." Jimmy shielded his eyes from sunlight so powerful, it felt like it had weight.

"Blessing and curse. You'll notice that you're not sweating, though?"

Jimmy looked at his hands. Dry as a Saltine. "Well, I'll be…"

"Desert heat, my friend. It's not even as hot as it gets. Tomorrow's supposed to hit a hundred-ten."

"Degrees?"

"Yup. You're actually sweating, but the second it hits your pores it evaporates. Can be quite dangerous. I've got some spring water in the car. You'll want to make sure that you stay hydrated."

Norm drove himself a brand new Beemer convertible. Not too bad for a real estate shill. Norm leaned over, popped the glove compartment and handed a bottle of water to Jimmy. "Here you are, pal." Norm started the car and Frank Sinatra immediately sprang from the speakers singing "My Way." "Welcome to Vegas, Jimmy. Believe you me; you live the life for a while, you may never leave."

Funny that, Jimmy thought, *I have no intention of leaving.*

After he checked into his room, Jimmy went to the lobby and asked about rates. Four-hundred a week. Unbelievable. In New York, Jimmy knew people who paid three times that to share a Bronx studio with a ten pound rat named Bruno. The complex was geared towards conventioneers, but what the hell. It had a friggin' pool. Jimmy paid the guy a month's advance and hit the tables, looking to build his kitty.

Before the clock turned the day over, Jimmy was forced to give up his first Vegas dream of becoming a career gambler. Three hours in the casino and his pot was already down five hundred between the craps and blackjack tables. Not long after his final double-down implosion, Jimmy was filling out an application in the casino bar for poker dealer. Work had never exactly been Jimmy's favorite four-letter word, but all he had to do to stay positive was to remind himself that he was alive and 2,500 miles away from Jonathan Bass' pointy things.

"Rise and shine Jimmy," came Norm's cheerful voice from behind the door.

Jimmy's eyes sprung open. He sat bolt-upright out of another nightmare (pointy, pointy). Then his stomach sat bolt-upright. While the rest of Jimmy found its bearings, his stomach went on to do the Worm, the Slide, the Twist and every other dance move Wilson Pickett sung about.

First night in Vegas, Jimmy had allowed himself a couple of drinks. The price was right in his new budget, in that they were comped. A couple turned into God-knows how many. Even skunk drunk as he was from the free table liquor, Jimmy managed to charm the phone numbers off two women he'd struck up conversations with. He was too shitfaced to entice them back to his room, but he'd be damned if the old Jimmy Romance magic wasn't still strong as ever.

Jimmy opened the door too quickly, then stumbled back as the heat and blinding sunlight smacked into him again. That shit was going to take some getting used to. It also felt like unbelievable torture on his hangover.

"Whoa," said Norm. "Looks like somebody tasted a bit too much of the old Vegas high life last night." Norm cackled and Jimmy fought the desire to unpack his gun and put an end to the high-pitched torture. "Listen," he said, "I'll go get some breakfast and be back in an hour. You think you'll be ready?"

"Yeah," Jimmy mumbled through dry and cracked lips. "Super."

Jimmy took the coldest shower of his life, hoping to wash the hangover away. He stood under the freezing jets with an empty coffee cup, repeatedly filling it under the stream and chugging it back into his dehydrated self. When he was done, he felt a little better, but his schlong had crawled halfway up his sternum.

When he pulled a shirt out of his bag, Jimmy looked at the revolver he'd packed just in case. He'd disassembled it and packed each piece into a different item, but it was still a minor miracle that the TSA hadn't dragged him off and turned him into a sock puppet for a few hours just for the attempt.

Luck.

Jimmy Romance was feeling it, brother. Long as he could suppress the memory of the previous nights' bad streak at blackjack, it was all coming up roses. He was gonna make it work.

He was heading out the door when he looked at the gun on the bed again. His problems were gone. What did he need the gun for now? Jimmy stopped at the door again.

Looked back at the gun.

Just in case.

The hard sell started the second Norm pulled onto the highway. Jimmy had trouble keeping his eyes open.

"Fortune Estates is going to be the premiere..." Jimmy's eyes drifted shut. "...golf courses accessible from the property."

Closing again.

Asleep.

Jimmy jumped up with a start at the hand on his shoulder.

"Whoa, whoa, there cowboy. Didn't mean to scare you," Norm said, his hands held up in mock-defense.

"Where are we?" They weren't even on any road to speak of anymore. All Jimmy could see on three sides was desert. Directly in front of the car was a ramshackle construction site. A couple of empty bulldozers were parked at the lip of what looked like a half-dozen empty foundations.

"The future site of Fortune Estates." Norm held his arms wide, like he was introducing Adam to the Garden of Eden.

Todd Robinson

"Nothing here," Jimmy croaked. His throat felt like it was full of dry ash. He went to get a bottle of water, but the glove compartment was locked.

"Nothing yet," Norm said, reaching into the back seat. He handed Jimmy a plastic gallon of Poland Spring. "Truth is, you're the first potential buyer we've brought here. We weren't planning on showing the site for another month. Been waiting for the weather to cool off a bit, but your circumstances made us bump up the schedule."

Jimmy sucked hungrily at the water, his head pounding a rumba. This was why he didn't drink.

"That wasn't fair of you," Norm said with a wink.

"What wasn't?"

"Sleeping through my pitch." Norm gave Jimmy another toothpaste ad smile. "C'mon. Let's go see the construction."

The desert wasn't what Jimmy expected. The ground had a gravelly consistency, like the stuff they poured in the infield at Jimmy's old Little League park. He was expecting more of a beach-type sand. There were no pointy cacti, just a lot of scrub. Scrub, gravel, and not a lot more. Jimmy stared down into one of the eight-foot deep foundations. His foot skidded in the sand and Norm grabbed Jimmy by the shoulder.

"Don't want to fall in there. It might be just sand, but that first step's a doozy." Norm haw-hawed.

Jimmy forced a smile. Yeah, a doozy. Me breaking my neck is real funny, too. He started feeling the old paranoia creeping back. There he was, literally in the middle of nowhere. The sensation was somehow sharpened to a point (pointy, pointy!) in the desert. The city kid inside him screaming for some concrete, one skyscraper to base perspective from. The sickness in the pit of his stomach was familiar, but the sweats were missing. Where were the sweats? Oh yeah. Sucked off by the hot air. Even his familiar fear felt wrong in this overheated death hole.

He'd tuned out Norm as they walked around the big nothing. What was wrong? There wasn't anybody who knew he was there. There was no place for anybody to hide. It was just the two of them, the open desert and...

And...

And a lot of holes in the ground.

"...right back." Norm said.

"Huh?"

"I said I'll be right back. I want to go get something in the car." Norm smacked Jimmy on the shoulder and trotted off. "Don't fall in."

It all came to him in a rush. Was it just a fucking coincidence that the offer came just at the right time? Jimmy hadn't been offered any timeshares before in his life. The thoughts bounced around Jimmy's brain like a superball. Butcher Bass had connections. Connected connections. Connections to crime.

Sin City.

Mean Gene. Mean Gene was getting a head start on his vacation tan. In Paris? Who the fuck went tanning in Paris?

In April.

There was, however, a casino called Paris right here in Vegas, the town hot enough to suck the moisture right off your bones.

Sin City, baby.

Jimmy watched Norm open the passenger door and lean down.

He was unlocking the glove compartment.

Jimmy didn't think Norm was getting mittens in the 110-degree heat.

For the first time since he'd arrived, Jimmy felt sweat on his neck as the rest of his body went numb. Without a second thought, he pulled his gun from the back of his pants and fired three shots into the windshield. The windshield splintered with a sound that reminded him of the one that Ricardo's face made when he slammed the tanning bed on it. Norm's outline bucked once and slumped over. Jimmy sucked the furnace air in rapid gulps. A couple of breaths later, his throat was squeaking dryly.

He started shuffling over to the car when the engine turned. Jimmy started running (to hide where exactly?) and emptied the gun at the shiny Beemer as it surged forward. The windshield exploded. The huge car didn't get far. It rolled into one of the empty foundations with a boom that echoed in the desert's empty expanse. The car's rear wheels kept rolling even though they had no ground to roll against anymore.

Jimmy jumped into the ditch, gun ready. He didn't realize that he'd emptied the clip in his panic, but it didn't matter. "Kill me, huh? You think you're gonna sucker Jimmy Romance? *Fuck you!*"

Jimmy opened the door. Norm's body lay still in the wheel well. Blood spurted from the puncture in his neck where one of Jimmy's bullets hit home, the tan linen jacket quickly going to red. Jimmy rolled him off the pedals onto the hardened foundation floor. Once his body was off the accelerator, the engine slowed, coughed once and died.

Norm's mouth moved like a dummy who'd lost his ventriloquist. Tears rolled down from eyes that weren't looking at anything in particular. Then with one heaving gasp, he was still.

Jimmy once-overed the car's interior. No gun.

With a loud crack, the wall of the foundation gave under the Beemer's weight and came crashing down. The car rolled onto its roof, over Norm's body with a wet crunch.

Good thing he's already dead, Jimmy thought. Now it was his turn to laugh, even though the sound of it was alien in his ears. Jimmy carefully climbed into the compacted luxury car and looked in the glove box.

Jesus, it's stifling.

He found blueprints, a contract and a smashed bottle of sparkling wine. Cheap bastard couldn't even spring for the good stuff. On the roof of the car (now the floor) lay two jugs of water. One was empty, a ragged bullet hole through the plastic. The other was intact, but more than half empty, since Jimmy had greedily drank from it only recently.

No gun. No knives. Hell, there wasn't even a toenail clipper in the car.

How do people live in this heat?

Jimmy climbed out the car and considered his options. They weren't bad. Yeah, he'd killed the guy, but it already looked like an accident. It wouldn't take much to torch what was left and let any evidence burn up.

The feeling of freedom washed over Jimmy again. He would get away with it. Sorry Norm, but there just wasn't any motive. Jimmy grabbed the bottle of water and walked over to the partially-collapsed foundation wall. He could climb over, follow the tire tracks, flag a car and sob his story to the cops.

As Jimmy tried pulling himself over the edge, his feet kept sinking into the loose earth. Skidding backwards, Jimmy fell ass-over-teakettle, the desert gravel crumbling through the now fully-collapsed wall. Sand and dust quickly poured in to fill the vacuum. Jimmy sat up, spitting out grit from between his teeth.

Jimmy rinsed the dry earth from his mouth, dusted off his pant legs. So the collapsed wall was a bust. No biggie.

Jimmy went to the other side and tossed the jug over the edge ahead of him. Jumping up, he grabbed the wall and scrabbled to get his leg over. The rim came free under his shoe, sending Jimmy tumbling onto his back, clutching two handfuls of foundation wall.

Jimmy crumbled the cheap concrete between his rolling fingers. Looked like the people building Fortune Estates were going to make their fortunes by cutting back on materials.

North and south walls, same goddamn thing.

He couldn't get out.

Damn, it was hot. Jimmy looked at his arms, which were already going a dangerous shade of red. He checked his watch.

11:42 a.m.

It was only going to get hotter.

Jimmy climbed onto the overturned car, tried to get up speed and flung himself towards the edge. He hit the lip of the foundation halfway over and slid back slowly into the hole, his fingers scraping over the all-too-yielding ground. Almost made it, until the fingernail on his left pinky finger ripped out. Jimmy fell onto his ass once more and screamed his curses into the air.

In frustration, he marched over Norm's corpse and kicked him in his dead face. *Too bad you're dead, Norm. I could have used the number for your manicurist.*

The second time, Jimmy tried to psyche himself up. This was the only way he was going to get out. Do or die. Now or never. The old Brooklyn try.

On the second step of his second attempt, Jimmy's ankle caught under the muffler. His shin snapped like a chopstick as he face-planted into a muddy pool of Norm's blood. Jimmy rolled back and forth in Norm's gore, howling in obscene pain at the merciless sun.

The sun didn't care.

Jimmy closed his eyes, steeling himself against the pain. A shadow flickered over his clenched eyelids. Jimmy opened his eyes. A few seconds later, the shadow returned.

Huh, thought Jimmy. *Would you look at that? Don't see too many of those back home.*

Nope. Of all the negative things he could say about New York, one thing it had going for it was that there were no buzzards in Brooklyn.

Angelo Death

For the third time in a week, Joe Shannon prays for death. In the quiet of his private room at Brigham and Women's Cancer Center, all he has for company is the quiet machine noises of his IV unit and the occasional groan from one of the other rooms down the hall.

hissssss-click

hissssss-click

Joe looks at the clock on the wall. 3:87 in the morning. He hasn't been able to sleep for more than two hours at a clip in a month and a half and he's tired.

He's tired of the pungent smell in his nose from the oxygen tubes.

He's tired of the same four walls.

He's just plain tired.

Wait a minute. 3:87 in the morning makes no sense. He squints at the clock again. 3:37—that made more sense. Goddamn Decadron screwing up the works in his brain.

Or maybe it was the Velcade.

Or maybe the Oxycontin.

Or the Vicodin.

Or maybe one of the other forty-nine pills that he was taking over the course of each day. Hell, the pills tasted better than the rotten hospital food they tried shoveling down his gullet. His doctors were concerned that he wasn't eating enough. How much could a man eat with a belly full of pills?

hissssss-click

hissssss-click

Joe adjusts the pillow under his swollen legs. Every pill in North America, and they didn't have one that could make his legs comfortable.

So tired.

His daughter visited from New York last week with the kids. It was nice until she started crying an hour into the visit and couldn't stop. It humiliated Joe to not be able to comfort his daughter—to be so weak as to not even be able to tell her to shut the waterworks off. Worst of all, his grandsons were wearing Yankees hats. Talk about insult to injury.

Well, soon enough he'd be able to apologize to Ted Williams and Tony Conigliaro himself. He just doesn't know when.

hissssss-click

hissssss-click chikchikhissssssss

Joe opens his eyes to make sure the IV machine wasn't going on the fritz again. The amount of money his family was paying for him to be in here, you'd thing those prick doctors would give him some machinery that worked.

As he turns his head, he sees that it isn't the machine, but the hydraulic door hinge opening.

In the dim light, he sees a tall man he doesn't know in an expensive-looking black suit. His skin is bone-white, a blood-red tie knotted over a black shirt.

In a gentle voice, he says, "Hello, Joe."

"Nurse! Nurse!" Joe shouts hoarsely, his voice dry and squeaky from panic and disuse. He strains weakly against the weight of his own atrophied muscles. He doesn't know the guy, but he knows why he's here. His hand finds the call button and he frantically presses the alarm. Distantly, he hears a bell chiming at the night nurse's desk.

"Joe, calm yourself. Don't get your tubes all tangled up."

"NURSE!"

"You're not making this any easier on yourself."

"And I'm not going to, you son of a bitch. You bastards aren't content to let me go out on my own terms?" Joe points the buzzer at his guest and presses the button.

"Knock yourself out." The guy straightens out his coat and sits in the hard plastic chair next to the bed. Casually, he pulls out a gold cigarette case.

Joe hears the squeaking of the nurse's shoes on the linoleum down the hallway. He laughs dryly. "You missed your chance, buddy. When that nurse gets here, she's gonna call the cops. You got about five seconds to get the fuck gone."

Slowly, the guy shakes his head. "I'm not going anywhere, Joe."

The nurse bursts through the door, flipping on the too-bright fluorescents. Joe is momentarily blinded. The nurse also blinks rapidly in the sudden harshness. As far as he can tell, the visitor doesn't react at all—either to the light or to the nurse's presence.

The night nurse is slightly out of breath. She's a sweet, pudgy little thing wearing a cheap engagement ring and a perpetually forced smile. Through the smile, she says, "What's wrong, Mr. Shannon? Why are you yelling?"

Her eyes never so much as glance over to the dapper stranger, who smiles at Joe and shrugs, cigarette dangling. He sparks a lighter and touches the flame to the tip of the cigarette. "She can't see me, Joe."

"I...I want that man out of the hospital. Call the police."

The nurse looks around the room. Her smile doesn't falter, but the strain of maintaining it clearly increases. "I'm sorry?"

"She can't hear me either."

Joe sits up, pointing at the man clearly sitting next to his bed. "Him! This greaseball bastard is here to kill me!"

The nurse's smile wavers a bit and her eyebrows knit up in sympathy. "There's nobody here, Mr. Shannon."

The visitor smiles and blows a perfect smoke ring. "Told ya."

"What?"

Simultaneously, the nurse and the visitor repeat themselves.

"I said, I told ya."

"I said, there's nobody here. You were just having a nightmare, Mr. Shannon. I've been at the desk all night and nobody has come by."

"But...but..." Despite himself, Joe feels a hot humiliation spreading through his chest. The finger he's pointing at the stranger shakes a little.

"And please don't yell any more. The other patients are trying to sleep. You should too." With that, the constant smile is planted back firmly where it belongs. The room plunges into semi-darkness again as she turns the light off and leaves the room.

The only sounds in the room...

hissssss-click

hissssss-click

Joe stares at the stranger. He closes his eyes and rubs at them. When he opens them again, the man is still there, calmly smoking.

"I'm still here, Joe," he says gently.

"Goddamn meds. Got me so looped up..." He hadn't had one yet, but Dr. Singh had told him that mild hallucinations were a possibility. There was nothing mild about his hallucination, Joe thought. He could see the type of knot the guy wore on his tie (Windsor). He could smell the cigarette smoke.

As if reading his thoughts, the man says, "I'm not a hallucination."

Joe chuffs. "Well, if you're the tooth fairy, you're a couple decades too late. My dentures are in the glass by the nightstand."

The man laughs warmly. "Not quite. I'll give you another guess, though."

Joe slumps his head back onto the stiff hospital pillow. "I'm outta guesses, buddy. So why don't you just tell me who you are?"

He takes one last drag off the filter and drops the butt into the miniature ginger ale can with a sizzle. "I'm the Angel of Death, Joe."

hissssss-click

hissssss-click

hissssss-click

"You gotta be kidding me."

"I'm afraid not. It's your time, my friend."

"Really? Where's your black robe? That sickle thing?" Joe is laughing hard now. It hurts, but it feels good, too. "Why do you look like every wop button man I ever met in my life?"

Death smiles at him. "Did you imagine that I would come to you in a black robe? Carrying a… I believe it's called a scythe."

"To be honest with you, I never imagined it at all. I dunno, I just always imagined it was…I dunno. Lights out and that was it."

"That's not entirely true. There were many times when you thought that someone—someone who looks like me—was going to end your life."

"What are you talking about?"

"1974?"

Joe narrows his eyes. "How do you know about that?"

"I know all about you, Joe. You and Sal Bustimante had quite the dispute about who was supposed to be paying who?"

Joe is silent. In shock.

"You thought that he might send some, excuse me, 'wop' to take care of you." Death makes a pistol from his thumb and forefinger and fires it, making a pop with his lips.

"Yeah. I was real scared."

"And there was Nino Valleta in '81"

"Hey, Mr. Death Big Shot. I didn't have anything to do with Nino disappearing. You know so much, why don't you know that, huh?"

Death smiled. "I do know that, Joe. I also know that you were terrified that Mr. Bustimante would hold you responsible—and again, that someone like me would come sneaking up behind you on Boylston. Your strongest visions of your own death have always been someone like me, Joe. That's why I'm here like this." He splays his hands wide, presenting himself.

"So you--"

"I appear in whatever form of death the near-deceased have always feared."

"You gotta be kidding me."

"You already said that, Joe"

"Sorry. But I can't be the first man on earth to call bullshit on you."

Death smiles. "Not everybody knows who I am, what I am when they see me. I don't often have to explain myself."

"What do you mean?"

I've been a lot of things over the years. I've been jealous husbands. Drug dealers selling the last hits. I've been dogs—hell, once I was a Buick Electra."

Joe can't help but laugh, doubling over when he does. Half from the humor he now sees in it all and half from the pain that the laughter generates in his ruined stomach. But he doesn't care. One way or the other, he knows it will all be over soon.

"What's so funny?"

"I...I'm kinda mad at myself for never imagining that I would get banged to death by Charlie's Angels. Instead I get you—freakin' Angelo Death." Joe wipes away the tears that are streaming from his eyes.

Death laughs again. "That's a good one. Don't know how much *I* would have enjoyed that scenario."

Despite the broken glass roiling in his stomach, Joe can't suppress his whoops of laughter. "Stop it, you're killing me."

Death's laughter subsides. He clears his throat and smiles wanly, sadly. "Yeah, that's what I'm doing, Joe." Death taps a finger to his nose.

"Little on the mark there, huh?" Joe finally gets his giggles under control, but the tears won't stop rolling down his face. It feels like the force of his laughter has chipped something else loose.

Quietly, Death says, "What's the matter, Joe?"

"I dunno. It's...I never got to make right." Joe points up towards the heavens. "Y'know? I never...I never got to make Confession or nothing."

"Are you sorry for the things you've done? Are you truly sorry for the life you've led?"

Joe thinks about it, trying to associate the acts most vivid in his memory to an emotional response within himself. He's a little surprised at what he finds. "Y'know what? I am."

Death stands up and opens his suit jacket. With one hand, he reaches in. With the other, he points upward and smiles. "Then He knows, too."

Joe turns his head into the antiseptic smelling pillow and closes his eyes. "I'm sorry. I don't want to see."

"You don't have to. Goodbye, Joe."

"Goodbye."

hisssss-click

hisssss-click

hisssss-click

hisssss-click

Joe Shannon smiles, even though his tears are still flowing.

hiss-pop

And the pain is over.

The visitor buttons his coat back up and walks out of the room. He stops at the nurse's station. "You received the money?"

"Yes sir. Thank you." The pasted smile never moves.

"And tell your fiancée that he's clear of his debts."

"Yes sir."

"You know what I have to do?"

"Yes sir."

"Close your eyes."

She does. The man in the black suit winds up and delivers a vicious punch to the nurse's temple. She crumples to the floor, unconscious, blood streaming along her hairline from the gash his ring made—a convincing enough injury.

He drives back to Southie, parks in front of an Irish Shebeen called Conor's. He knows they'll be in the back room. The red-haired hostess nods at him as he passes. He walks through the kitchen into the room marked Employees Only.

Five old men are seated around the poker table, cards and chips in front of them. One of them has an oxygen tank strapped to his wheelchair.

hissssss-click

The passage of time hasn't been much kinder to the other four. One holds his cards with knobby fingers ravaged by arthritis. Three of them look up at him with glasses thicker than storm windows.

"Is it done?" one asks, his voice still tinged with the light brogue he brought to Boston fifty years earlier from Galway.

"It's done."

The man in the wheelchair starts to weep softly. Arthritis-Fingers lays an arm over his withered shoulders. "He was suffering, Seamus."

"I know. I know." He takes a deep breath, blows it out with a shudder. "It's a good death."

"Damn right," says another old-timer. "Joe Shannon deserved to go out like a man. Not wasting away in cheap hospicthckkk-" The old-timer's dentures catch on the sibilants and are halfway out his mouth before he catches them. "Gawdammit."

Those who can do so, stand. They all raise their glasses towards one of their own. "We'd like to thank you, Mr. Bustimante, for letting us use your man for this."

Sal Bustimante raises his glass of red wine into the air. He's met with four pints of Guinness. "*Agli amici più con noi.* To friends no longer with us."

To friends no longer with us.

Delivery

"I got Northern Lights, Grape Ape, Kryptonite, Silk, White Rhino, White Widow, Emerald Gold, Bubble Gum and Double Bubble," Jamie said to the skinny doe-eyed girl leaning on the doorjamb of her apartment.

She bit her lip nodding, mulling over her options. "Don't you have any more of that Kush I got last week?"

"Was Kush in that long list I just recited?"

The girl blinked, confused by the question. "I don't remember."

Jamie gritted his teeth. "It wasn't." Goddamn potheads. Their short-term memory was more often than not blown to the four winds anyhow. Hell, his own wasn't much better. Even though he could feel his patience burning away with the girl, Jamie appreciated the reprieve from the chill fall rain outside..

"Oh. I liked that one. Real mellow smoke." The girl nodded into her statement, like a pecking bird.

"Might have some next week."

"Got any G-13?"

Despite the fact that Jamie hadn't included the pharmaceutical grade strain in his list, he always carried two packets, in case. He just didn't think that this girl, answering the door in her beat up U-Mass sweatshirt, had the scratch to buy the stuff. It was the premier, top of the line weed ever produced. Thank you, Uncle Sam. "Yeah. It's a hundred-fifty."

"Whoa."

He knew it. He'd delivered to this girl four times in the last month and had never sold her anything better than Kryptonite or Kush. None too expensive. She acted like he was one of the Fenway hustlers who sold teenagers baggies cut with oregano. Jamie only sold weed rated from really good up to G-13, but the girl obviously had no idea what the hell she was talking about. "Try the Silk. The high is pretty close."

"To the G-13?" Her eyes widened in hope.

"No, to Kush. Nothing is close to G-13. If there was, you couldn't afford it."

"Fuck you, I can afford it." The girl bobbed her head in an attitude more appropriate for a guest on *Maury* than college student. From bird to trailer trash in one neck swivel.

Jamie was tired of the exchange. He wanted to make the sale and get out of Dodge. He didn't need to get into an argument with the twit about her budget. "Listen, you buying today, or not?"

"Give me the Silk."

"Fifty." Jamie reached into his pocket and drew out the small bag. The girl handed him a rolled-up mess of singles and fives. She held her hand out impatiently.

"Wait," Jamie ordered as he unfolded the bills and counted. The girl sighed with annoyance. Jamie was ready to chuck the money in her face and walk, if Hugh wouldn't chew him out for blowing a sale. Fifty even. Thank God, Jamie thought as he slapped the bud into her hand. She made no effort to close the door gently.

Bitch.

Jamie waited at Model Bar for his next call, sipping a Heineken. Most days, he didn't mind riding his bike. Some of the other couriers on Hugh's payroll bought themselves scooters or dirt bikes to motor around in. Jamie still liked riding his bicycle. It was slower than anything motored, but not by much. On his bike, he could still choose which traffic laws to obey, which lights to run, any route he wanted. The guys on motors had to be double careful not to catch the cop's attention. That was one thing Jamie was good at. On the street, he was the Flash, the Invisible Man and Keyser Soze all rolled into one. You think he's there and poof...gone.

Except in the rain. And it was cold. Summer rain wasn't so bad, could even be refreshing, but this crap just flat-out sucked. From his messenger bag he pulled out one of his old man's ancient Travis McGee books to pass the time, but the rain had warped the pages. The cigarette-yellowed paper stuck together, making it impossible to read. Jamie thought he could still smell the old man's Camels between the wet pages.

Then his cell phone rang.

"Yeah"

"22 Cabot Street. Roxbury."

"Dammit, Hugh. Don't be sending me to Roxbury in this weather." Jamie thought; *Don't send me to Roxbury at all*, but didn't say it. The day could have been sunshine and kittens, Roxbury was still a shit run.

"Bring the G-13."

"What? Aw, hell no. Have you looked outside?"

"Apartment 2-E." Click. Hugh didn't argue, much less with his employees. You made the delivery, or you returned to the base, handed over your stash, and never returned.

Jamie was aware of his place. Yeah, he was a scumbag drug dealer, but he was positive nobody ever O.D.ed on what he sold. Gateway drug, my ass. Jamie smoked weed regularly since he was old enough to roll and he never felt the urge to upgrade his high.

Yeah, Jamie knew his place. Knew the game, and he didn't like rolling his dice in that neighborhood. Suddenly,

Jamie was appreciative of the freezing rain. In better weather, nearly every corner in Roxbury had a crew on it. They weren't necessarily Crips or Bloods, but those guys were out there too, mostly dealing themselves. Sometimes looking for the next sucker to jack. All of them dangerous. Even though they tended to deal exclusively on the higher-potency end of the drug spectrum—crack, horse, coke— they didn't appreciate Jamie and the other couriers on their turf. They'd throw bottles as he sped by, calling out "Hey White Boy!"

Jamie got jumped once on the lip of Roxbury. That night, some gangbangers recognized him from return trips and mugged him. Only they weren't content with a simple robbery. Jamie spent three weeks hospitalized, a month before he could get on a bike again. Hugh, not offering any health plan, was decent enough to cover Jamie's hospital costs. The lost merchandise and money came out of Jamie's pocket, though.

The one time Hugh visited him, his condolences were, "Watch your back next time."

Jamie didn't respond. One, his back wouldn't have mattered. They'd swarmed him from all sides. Two, his jaw was wired.

22 Cabot didn't look like too bad a building for the hood. Like having a skybox in Hell, Jamie thought.

The inside was another matter. The checkered floor looked like it hadn't been washed in years and Lord, the smell—cooking odors, sharp spices mixed with a stench of wet decay that made Jamie's stomach churn.

Jamie pinched his nose walking up the stairwell. Somebody was yelling in Russian. Another had their television turned way loud. Alex Trebek said, *"Monticello."*

Who the hell would be living in this dump and buying G-13? Maybe somebody called and they were going to rob him again, knowing he was going to be carrying the best stuff.

He had no choice. Make the delivery or be out of a job. Some of the other guys armed themselves, and for a moment, Jamie reconsidered his negative stance on carrying a weapon. But in the event of a po-po shake, he didn't need weapons possession added to the charges he would already be carrying in his messenger bag. He though about bringing his bike chain with him, but shit, leave his bike unchained? In Roxbury?

Besides, he knew his capabilities. Jamie wasn't a brawler, but he could run, given the right reasons. And once he was on his bike, he was gone.

2-E. Jamie knocked. He heard rustling inside and a deadbolt click. The door opened a crack and a small Hispanic woman peeked out. "Can I help you?" she asked softly. Her voice was tinged with an accent. What Jamie could see was pretty as hell. The eye in the crack was a deep brown, long lashes.

For a second, Jamie forgot what he was there for. "Uh, yeah. Delivery?"

"You bring pizza?" She peeked a little further and looked at Jamie's empty hands.

"Huh?" This had never happened before. Jamie looked at the door number again. Somebody screw up the apartment numbers? "No, I..."

"Jen! Who you talkin' to?" a male voice yelled behind her.

"Is a delivery," she replied.

Jen fell away from the door, pulled roughly back. "The fuck you doin' answering the door?"

Aw no... Jamie knew the voice. Fucking Trezza.

Trezza swung the door wide. He was shirtless, muscles twitching at Jamie. He'd grown a gut, but he was still huge. And all things equal, he was most likely still a psychopath, too. Through the door, Hugh could see into the apartment. Considering the building, the neighborhood and all, the apartment was clean. Big flat-screen. Furniture that didn't look like it had been picked off a curb.

"S'up?" said Trezza. "You one of Hugh's boys?"

"Yeah," Jamie said. Thank God for small favors. Trezza didn't recognize him. Not that there was any beef, but Jamie preferred anonymity where Jude Trezza was concerned. Jamie had delivered to Trezza a couple times, years ago when Trezza had a pad in Jamaica Plains. The guy was a nightmare.

"What you got?"

"I got Northern Lights…"

Trezza grabbed him and pushed him hard into the wall, held Jamie by the collar of his windbreaker. "I'm talkin' G-13, bitch. You think I can't afford the good shit? Save the skunk for the sororities, *bitch*."

Jamie's legs went weak, remembering what Trezza had done to Ike. "Yeah. I got two packets," Jamie croaked. He tried to keep the fear out of his voice, but heard it trembling anyway. Self-loathing coursed through Jamie. His nerves told him to run. His pride said fight back. The brain won. Fighting back would be suicide, at least more hospital time. Jamie wasn't eager for either.

Trezza smiled crookedly at Jamie. "You scared, Pee-Wee?" Jamie didn't have to respond. Trezza knew that he was. "You should be. You know what happened to the last guy tried to rip me off?"

Jamie nodded.

Trezza let his collar go. "Damn, only got two? I got my boys coming over. Two packets ain't gonna do it."

"I only got two."

"What's the next best?"

"Depends. Kryptonite and Silk are both…"

"Gimme it all." Trezza waved his hand and pulled a wad of hundreds from his pocket.

When Jamie went to his pack, he saw around Trezza's legs. Jen sat on the couch. She and Jamie locked eyes for a moment. Well, locked eye was more appropriate. Her left eye, the one that Jamie couldn't see through the crack was swollen shut. The biggest part of her was her stomach. She was really, really pregnant.

"What?" The sharpness of Trezza's tone snapped Jamie back. Again, he had no response. Trezza's gaze hardened as he looked back and realized just what Jamie was looking at. A backhand clipped Jamie across the face; lightly, but enough to humiliate him. "Mind your own."

Jamie noticed tracks in the crook of Trezza's elbow.

"I can't believe you sent me there." Jamie was pissed. Hugh knew Trezza's history. Not only was Trezza one of the biggest heroin dealers in Boston, but a year ago he beat down another member of Hugh's delivery crew. Jamie was pissed not only that they were still delivering to the prick, but that Hugh sent *him*.

Adding to that aggravation was Jamie's difficulty finding Hugh's new base of operations. Hugh kept his operation mobile, ever since four armed guys hit his place in Brighton. It was a righteous paranoia, but he'd forgotten to tell Jamie where he moved to. Jamie had to ride an extra hour in the rain while he tried to connect with Hugh in order to bitch at him. Hugh finally answered on Jamie's sixth attempt. Hugh didn't like being called. Hugh was the man who made the calls.

"Trezza's a customer." Hugh didn't look from his scale, carefully weighing out the packets.

"Ike..."

"Ike ripped him off. Conversely, he was ripping me off."

Ike thought he was clever, started selling fake G-13 in order to line his pockets beyond what Hugh paid him. Nobody knew how long Ike had been running the scam, but it came to an abrupt halt when Trezza busted him on the fake. That was over a year ago. Ike was still eating through straws. "He threatened me."

"How much did he buy?" That was going to be the checkmate. Louder than words, any threats made, the money would win, would always win. "Six hundred," Jamie mumbled.

"How much?" Hugh asked again, holding his hand against his ear for emphasis.

"Six hundred," Jamie said.

"'Nuff said." Hugh pinched off a small portion of pot from an enormous bag and placed it on the scale. He handed the baggie to Jamie. "Enjoy. Hazard pay. Smoke it when you get home and chill the fuck out, Jamie."

Jamie tried once more. "Looked like he's started hitting his own goods."

Hugh's attention had already returned to the task at hand. "Don't care."

Jamie rode for as long as he could, trying to push his emotions out through the pedals. The anger just moved through his body as he shot through traffic. It was getting dark before Jamie headed home to Southie. He let himself in through the basement door, rather than track moisture over his mother's rugs. The last thing he needed was a hissy fit from his mother about not being able to have nice things. Nice things being the ten-dollar Oriental rug runner purchased twenty years ago from K-Mart.

"Jamie? That you?" His mother called down the stairwell. Jamie peeled off the wet clothes that stuck to him like Saran Wrap.

"No, Ma. It's a psycho, here to steal your Hummels."

"Don't be a smart-ass." When his mother was aggravated, her Southie accent deepened. Jamie could tell she was in a state when she called him "smaht-ass".

"What now, Ma?"

"Your dinner's almost cold."

"Yell at me when it's cold, then." It was Thursday. Shepherd's pie night in the McGowan house. It wasn't very good when it was hot. Jamie's mother suffered from the culinary challenges that faced generations of Boston's Irish.

Jamie heard her mutter another "smaht-ass" as she shuffled off. At least living in the basement afforded him some privacy. His mother's bad hip left her paranoid about tumbling down the stairs.

Jamie's mood didn't leave him with much of an appetite anyway. Instead, he rolled himself a small joint from Hugh's gift bag that he hoped would help his attitude and give him enough of the munchies to choke down his mother's cold shepherd's pie.

For a few weeks, he suffered mild paranoia whenever his phone rang. His gut clenched between answering and getting the address. He dreaded having to go back to Trezza's. After some time passed, so did his worries.

Four months later, Jamie was at the Model, like always, waiting on the next delivery. The phone chimed on the bar. "Where to, Hugh?"

"22 Cabot Street. Roxbury."

Jamie closed his eyes, took a shallow breath as the old fear crept back into his belly. "Aw, hell no, Hugh…" Jamie didn't want to whine, but he heard his voice squeak anyway.

"22 Cabot Street. Roxbury."

"C'mon, can't you…? Jamie cut the complaint short. Somewhere irrational, he hoped that it was another apartment. There was more than one in that shithole,

"Apartment 2-E." The phone disconnected.

The fear that washed over him when he walked out the door suddenly took a 180-degree turn into anger. Anger at his own cowardice, his weakness. Jamie threw his phone down onto the concrete. The plastic shattered and Jamie felt a small release. At least Hugh would have to buy him a new phone. That'll teach the prick to send him to Trezza's again.

Jamie rode as fast as he could to the address and ran up the stairs. The whole ride across town, Jamie convinced himself that it was better this way. Facing his fears, and all that Dr. Phil shit.

Hell, who was he kidding. He was scared shitless.

Jamie could smell it from the other end of the hallway. At first, he thought it must have been coming from somewhere else. The stench of diapers and pizza (that was all he could relate it to) was definitely coming from apartment 2-E. A quick edit of slasher films projected through Jamie's imagination.

The door opened wide this time. Jamie couldn't see anyone inside. Then he looked down.

A kid, no older than five, stood there, smiling up at him.

His Spongebob pajamas looked like they hadn't been washed in weeks. Jamie remembered Jen and her eye. The kid looked just like her, but the nose was Trezza's. Trezza had the type of nose that had obviously taken a few punches over the years.

So had the kid's.

Looking at the child flooded Jamie with unwanted memories of his old man and his own eager willingness to lash out. Staring at the boy's disfigured nose made the old scars on the back of Jamie's legs burn as though the leather had just whipped across them. He smoldered with an anger he'd thought long dead when the kid took Jamie's fingers and led him inside.

"Is your Daddy home?" Jamie felt like an asshole for even asking. For Christ's sake, he was there to sell Daddy drugs. In the months since Jamie had been there, the apartment had gone to the dogs. The kid pulled Jamie to the coffee table and opened a Cohiba box. For a second, Jamie thought the kid was offering him a cigar.

He wasn't.

A handful of unopened disposable hypodermics, matches, a spoon and packets of heroin sat in the box.

Jesus Fuck, the kid was offering him a hit.

He'd probably seen Daddy do it so many times that he'd adopted the gesture.

"Uh, no thanks," Jamie said through numb lips. *From watching you Dad. I learned it from watching you.* Jamie remembered the old anti-drug campaign and would have laughed if he wasn't so fucking horrified.

A toilet flushed and out walked Trezza. He'd dropped at least thirty pounds (which only meant that he still outweighed Jamie by about fifty), and looked...

Unwashed was the only word that came into Jamie's mind.

Trezza stopped buckling his belt when he saw what was happening at his stash. His eyes went wide and he charged Jamie like an enraged pitbull, driving him into the wall and knocking his wind out.

"The fuck you doing in my house? The fuck you doing with my box?" he screamed. Trezza's eyes were wild, darting all over Jamie, pupils burned down to fiery pinpricks.

"Nothing," Jamie wheezed, his lungs spasming.

"Who the fuck are you?" Trezza reached into his back pocket and pulled a box cutter. He flicked his thumb, opening the blade with a click. He pressed the tip to Jamie's throat. "Answer me!" Again, Trezza failed to recognize Jamie. This time however, Jamie wished he did.

"De-delivery," Jamie said hoarsely.

Don't let me pee. Please don't let me pee.

A small light of memory—either of Jamie or of the fact that he'd called for some weed—shone on Trezza's furious expression. "Asshole," was all Trezza said before he bashed Jamie on the nose with the bottom of his fist.

Blood gushed from Jamie's nostrils, filled his sinuses as he crumpled to the floor. "Don't ever let me see you in my house again." He turned to the kid. "And what the fuck are you doing?"

The kid was crying, pleading to Trezza in panicked Spanish. Jamie didn't understand anything the kid was saying except for "Papi"

Trezza brutally slapped his child, knocking him to the floor. The kid wailed, terrified and hurt, the blood from his busted lip seeping into the sleeve of his Spongebob pee-jays.

"Quit it!" Trezza raised his hand again and the boy scrambled under the coffee table, away from his father's fists. The kid balled up, his cries drawn into whimpers.

Trezza rifled Jamie's bag, looking at the packets. Taking what he wanted, he threw the backpack at Jamie, lifted him by the shirt and tossed him into the hallway. Trezza threw a wad of crumpled bills at Jamie's feet and slammed the door. Jamie then heard more yelling in Spanish. Trezza's voice, harsh and abusive. Jen's pleading. Jamie heard flesh smacking and more sobbing.

Then an infant's weak cries joined the din.

Jamie half-crawled, half-fell down the stairs as he fought to escape as fast as he could.

"Jamie, please... What's wrong?" Jamie's mother hovered at the top of the stairs. She'd heard Jamie when he came in. Probably because when he did, he'd lost control and thrown his bike across the room. It landed on with a crash that could probably be heard downtown, much less upstairs. His mother started crying when she heard the tears in Jamie's voice.

"Leave me alone, Ma!" Jamie couldn't stop crying. His nose wouldn't stop bleeding. It wouldn't stop. None of it would stop.

"Please, Jamie," she sobbed. "I can't help you. I can't come down there."

"Just go away, please." Jamie curled up on the musty carpet. Everything hurt.

Then his mother said, "I miss your Dad, too."

Jamie let her think that.

"You get the license number?" Hugh gave him the once-over as Jamie held ice against his swollen nose. Hugh, with his usual style, expressed slightly more sympathy than a brick.

Jamie shook his head. He would have said "no", but he was trying to avoid any words using the letter N. The sound sent bolts of pain into Jamie's nasal cavities. "Guy bumped me and jetted." The explanation worked for two reasons, since Jamie didn't have to come up with a second excuse to explain the busted phone.

"Doesn't look like you need stitches." Hugh was looking at the cut on the back of Jamie's head. Jamie guessed that he'd suffered it while tumbling down the stairs. He heard Hugh sigh with relief. Probably less in concern over Jamie than at the decreasing possibility that he'd have to foot another hospital bill. "You sure you don't want to get checked out? You might have internal injuries."

Jamie shook his head carefully, otherwise his nose might start leaking again. "I fell odd my head." Jeez, talking was difficult.

Hugh sighed, "Good. I mean…"

Jamie waved off Hugh's apology. "Weh he calls, I wah Drebba's delibbery."

"Huh?"

Jamie repeated himself, as best he could.

Hugh shrugged. "I'm not understanding you."

"Drebba!"

"Terror? What terror?"

Jamie grabbed a notebook off the desk. There was no way to say it without n's. He wrote on the paper: *When he calls, I want Trezza's delivery.*

Hugh read the note and smiled. "You two kiss and make up?"

Jamie shrugged. *Good tipper*, he wrote

It was raining again when Jamie went back to Cabot Street. Jamie's sneakers squished wetly on the stairs. The rank smell was worse this time. It had been three months since Trezza broke Jamie's nose. It healed badly, leaving him a lump on the bridge and unable to smell through his left nostril. The closer he got to 2-E, the more he wished that neither one was operational. Before he got to the door, Jamie opened his backpack and put the baggie in his pocket. He didn't know if the opportunity would arise, but he'd waited three months. Too long to not be ready.

He knocked.

Nothing.

He knocked harder. Jamie's heart picked up the pace, but not from fear this time.

"Who izzit?" came a slurred voice from the other side.

"Delivery," was all he said, flat-voiced.

"Open the fuggin' door,"

Jamie slowly opened the door and poked his head in.

"Bout time," said Trezza. He looked like he'd dropped another thirty pounds. The once intimidating frame looked like somebody had made a Jude Trezza scarecrow and carelessly threw it onto the couch.

Jamie fought off the violent rush he felt course through him. For once in his life, he might have had the upper hand physically. Jamie remained calm, he would stick to the plan.

"Gimme the weed," Trezza said, his eyes half-lidded.

Jamie walked over and placed the packet onto the table, next to the cigar box.

With difficulty, Trezza drew a significantly smaller wad of cash from his pocket. For a second, he stared at his hand like he wondered how the money got there.

"How much?" Trezza drooled onto his lips and wiped it with his forearm. The tracks made a connect-the-dots game, mapping out the veins on his arm.

"Fifty for what's there."

"Fuck. Fifty bucks for pencil shavings," he muttered. Trezza slapped the bills into Jamie's palm.

Jamie needed to buy some more time. "Can I use your phone?"

"The fuck for?"

"Battery died on my cell. I gotta call Hugh."

Trezza waved towards an old brown plastic phone on the end table. "Whatever."

Jamie picked up the phone and dialed.

"...at the tone, the exact time will..."

"Yeah, Hugh. It's me."

"...beeeeeeeeeeeeeeeep..."

Trezza stood and stumbled to the bathroom.

Jamie hung up and opened the cigar box. He pulled the baggie from his pocket and compared. He held the two side-by-side. The color was right. Jamie added cinnamon to the Clorox before bagging it. He placed his bag into the box. There was more in Jamie's bag, but he doubted that Trezza would notice or care. If there was less, Jamie had no doubt that repercussions would come crashing down on Trezza's family.

On his way to the door, Jamie noticed the empty crib.

And Jen staring at him through the kitchen doorway.

Her eyes flickered to the cigar box, then to the hand that Jamie palmed the real heroin in.

Almost imperceptibly, she nodded, then walked back to whatever she was stirring on the stove.

The toilet flushed and Jamie dropped the heroin on the floor. It landed next to a tiny foot in a Spider-Man sock. He bent quickly to pick it up and saw the little boy in his hiding place under the coffee table. The boy put a finger to his lips. Jamie winked as he stuck the drugs into his pocket. Then he held his own finger to his lips, smiling. The kid grinned and put his hand over his mouth to stifle the giggles.

Jamie was gone before Trezza made out from the bathroom.

The Saint of Gunners

I rolled down the window of my unremarkable rented Taurus outside Elvis's Lounge. The residual fumes from the half-pack I'd chained rose into the darkness like an urban smoke signal. Even though I was parked in behind a van, conveniently shadowed from the streetlights, the young idiot should have seen me from his position. For him, the entire world was focused down to a pinpoint onto the painted red door.

The kid was clearly too fired up to make even the most basic attempts at being inconspicuous. I was good enough at it. Others were better. The kid pacing nervously under the awning next to Elvis's was being so obvious, he might as well have been dressed in a gorilla suit and blowing an air horn.

I was testing him, giving him every chance in the world to go about his business without me sticking my nose in it.

He failed. Emotion was making him stupid. Or worse, it was going to get him killed.

I had no intention of somebody else's idiocy having me killed along with him. Bullets don't discriminate when they start firing.

He was dressed in an oversized cream-colored jacket and a bright red Yankees cap that practically glowed under the light. This kid could be one of, if not the first person killed for making poor fashion choices. He was all boiling hot piss and vinegar. The readout on my dashboard said it was 17 degrees out. Even if it was the middle of July, he should have had gloves on if he intended to use the gun that he had in his right hand.

I sighed and crawled across the front seat of the car and exited on the passenger side, away from the street. I stuck to the shadows, taking the long route inside the glow of the streetlights. My soft-soled shoes made no sound as I worked my way up behind the kid. The last three feet behind him were well lit under the awning. I took those three feet fast as I pressed the muzzle of my revolver under his ear. The kid froze, arms by his side. The light gleamed off of the chrome piece in his hand. Even his gun conspired to give him away.

"You turn your head and the last thing you see will be your own face lying on the sidewalk. Say yes if you understand me."

"Y--yes." His frightened breaths froze in the air, his throat clicking as he swallowed.

"Good. Now hand me the gun slowly and walk backwards with me until we're out of these goddamn spotlights." Not too bad a gun; a Smith & Wesson Short .40, serial numbers filed off. Point one for the kid doing at least one thing right. We backed into the darkness and I stuck his gun into the back of my black jeans. "Now, you see the Taurus behind the van?"

"Yeah"

"Walk to it. Go around to the rear passenger side and get in."

Dutifully, he did as he was told. His gait was defiant. Not at all the walk of somebody with a gun at his back. Had to give the boy some credit. Mighty big stones for a kid that couldn't be any older than sixteen.

I climbed in behind him, pushing him along the seat with light pressure into his ribs with my gun. I would have preferred not to kill him in the rental car if I didn't have to. Rather not have to kill him at all. Too many bodies make for a messy night and a longer than usual explanation to my rental agent.

"You gonna smoke me?"

"That's all up to you, Sean."

"My name's not Sean."

"Well, since you got that name written all over your coat, let's just stick to that for right now."

The kid clucked his tongue. "That's the brand name, man."

I moved the barrel of my gun up to the base of his skull and pushed it hard, pressing his forehead against the glass. "Tell you what? The man with the gun says it's your name right now, unless you want to tell me what the real one is."

"Carlos."

"Now, Carlos, you mind telling me what you're doing marching back and forth next to Elvis Maxwell's joint with a gun?" I knew the answer; I just wanted to hear him speak it.

"I- I wasn't..."

"Wasn't what? Trying to get yourself killed? Making a mess of my night? Guess what, kiddo? Until I stepped in there, you were preparing to do both with blazing probability."

"How am I making a mess of *your* night?" Anger edged his words.

"I have business here."

"What business?"

"None of yours. But it's business that would best be conducted without your dumb ass raining gunfire and stupidity all over the place." I rapped him on the back of his head hard enough to just hurt him and knock that stupid Yankees cap off.

His breaths were becoming ragged. "You gonna kill me, then kill me." His voice was becoming thick, but not with fear.

Suddenly, I recognized the kid, knew why he was there.

Or, more accurately, I recognized his features. He looked just like his sister, the one who had been in the newspapers a couple weeks back. The one who used to work for Elvis taking coats at his club when she wasn't removing the rest of her clothing at the Blue Ruby. I'd read about the vicious drunken assault that happened inside the strip club. Heard more detail on whispered lips in the dark places I frequent. Whispers about who had done it to her and how she was too scared to point a finger.

"I'm not going to kill you. I'm giving you a chance to walk away here. I know what Elvis did to your sister. I know—"

"What do you know. What the fuck do you know, man?" he cried as he started turning towards me.

I moved the barrel over his eye, blocking his vision as I slid to my left, keeping out of his sight line. I didn't need any accidents that a panicking overemotional kid could easily cause. "Uh-uh-uh. You just face out, kid." Tears slid down his cheeks, rolled down the gunmetal.

"He's gotta pay, man. He's gotta pay..." he mumbled, more to himself than me as he turned his eyes back onto the door of the club.

"He is, but let the courts do their thing." The statement felt ludicrous coming out of my mouth, considering I had a gun to his face.

"You can't be serious. A man as mobbed up as Elvis Maxwell?"

"That's exactly what I'm saying. The Feds have been itching for something to put him away for."

"And you think that they're gonna care about some spic stripper he raped? He kills people. I ain't stupid."

"You are if you think he's gonna let you get within fifty feet of him without killing you first."

"Then what? He just going to get away with it?"

126

I thought about myself. All of my sins. My history of getting away with precisely that. "Nobody gets away with it in the end."

"That's bullshit, man. And you know it."

I didn't know if it was or it wasn't, but I said, "What isn't bullshit is that cab coming down the street. That's the cab that you're going to hail and go home in. Your sister needs you. She's got enough to deal with without her little brother dead from some half-assed attempt at payback. Be there for her." I stuffed a twenty into his coat pocket. "If you turn around, I put bullets in your spine. Got it?"

He sniffed and nodded his head low. "Got it."

"Now pick up your stupid hat and go home."

He opened the door and stuck his hand out. The yellow cab pulled up and he climbed in, never looking back. I waited until the taillights cornered Broadway before I got out of the car and strolled over to Elvis's. The club wouldn't be open yet, so I buzzed the bell by the huge metal door.

A Dominican guy with a shaved head and a neck thicker than the head opened the door. His other hand slid to his side, just out of vision, but at the ready. Very professional. He turned his huge neck, looking up and down the street. "Hey T.C."

"What's going on, Jesus?"

"That dummy in the Yanks cap split?"

"Yeah," I said. I looked at Jesus straight. "Benji called me. Said Elvis needed to see me."

"Elvis is waiting on you upstairs."

"Gotcha." Jesus did some freelance for Benji, just like I did. Benji was probably who assigned him the bodyguard detail on Elvis in the first place.

We eyeballed each other for a second. Professional respect and challenge in both our eyes. Two Alpha dogs who would forever wonder which one was Beta until such time they met in a pit. "We cool?" I asked.

Jesus shrugged his huge shoulders. It looked like boulders shifting under Armani. "Ain't no thang. Benji gave me the 411."

I walked past him, down the crimson velvet covered walls. Thumping dance music reverberated down the corridor. I turned left at the end and saw Elvis Maxwell sitting alone in a leather booth. He had on a purple wool suit and a white shirt, open at the collar. All he needed was a gold medallion and he would have looked like a disco lizard, time-warped from 1979.

He saw me and lifted a remote. The techno music cut off abruptly. The annoying bass line echoed in my ears for a couple seconds.

"Tee-SEE!" he yelled, my name echoing through the spacious emptiness. For a man who cherishes anonymity as much as I do, hearing my name not only yelled, but echoing, made the hair on my neck rise. He opened his arms wide, a brandy snifter in his hand, amber liquid sloshing at his gesture.

"Elvis," I said, considerably softer.

Elvis slicked his oily hair back with his fingers before he offered his handshake. Despite my disgust, I took it. The grease rolled around my fingers like I'd just eaten a cheap slice of pizza.

He popped a thin brown cigarette between his thin lips directly from the pack, then offered the pack to me.

"No thanks." I did want one, but couldn't stomach the thought of his lips touching one of the filters that might touch mine.

He shrugged. "Your choice. It's become decadent to smoke in my own fucking bar. You believe that? I can't even smoke in my own place?" He swirled the cognac in affectation before he tossed what remained down his gullet. "You have any idea how much money I put into this motherfucker? Next thing you know, they'll say you can't drink in a bar." He poured himself another healthy dollop of Frapin from the bottle out on the table. He chased the seven hundred dollar bottle of liquor with a can of Red Bull. Classy guy all the way.

"Times have changed."

"Ain't that some shit? Christ, just remembering when you could smoke in a bar makes me feel like a dinosaur. Who knew fucking Bloomburg would make Giuliani look like Caligula. During Rudy's days, I was still doing lines off of Ford Model titties. Now I can't even light a fucking Camel? Ain't that some shit?"

"Like I said. Times have changed." I sat down opposite him at the table. "So, what happened?"

He dismissed my question with a wave. "That's not important. What is..."

I interrupted him. "Actually, it is."

He glared hard at me. He wasn't used to being interrupted or challenged on what he considered to be his own turf. Thing about fuckwits like Elvis? They never seem to get that the turf they considered "theirs" was only due to the grace of God and the people who employ me. "You're kidding me, right?" His tone indicated that I might be.

I wasn't. I went on. "Do you know how money much the Gayden sisters have in The Blue Ruby?"

"C'mon, T.C., that run down little nudie bar?"

"Exactly. It's run down for a reason. The Yuens move a sizeable amount through there too."

"I know." He huffed a humorless laugh. "So imagine my surprise when that little spic whore calls the cops. She works here for me, playing the cockteasing princess in a mini-skirt. I go to Blue Ruby, and there she is, naked as a jaybird. She's cock hungry enough to take my money, to walk me into the fucking Champagne Room and rub her cootchie all over my cock, then she's gonna bitch when Lil' Elvis comes out to play?"

"She said you raped her, beat her after the lapdance."

"That's not the point."

"What is then?"

"I need you to take care of her. That's why I called Benji. Benji calls you. You getting my drift?" His attitude was shifting from appreciative to smarmy. A little man with a little power.

"Nobody wanted the police poking around The Ruby. You should have known better."

He stood up sharply, red impatience creeping up his neck. "You listen to me, and you listen to me right now. You are hired fucking help and no more. I ain't paying for your fucking opinion on what I do and do not fucking know. You hear me?" Two fingers curled around the snifter, stabbing his anger at the air in front of me.

I placed my hands on my lap, listening to him without expression.

"You get paid to take care of this shit, and nothing more." He took a manila envelope held together by a thick rubber band from inside his jacket pocket. "You're a tool. An employee, at best. If I hand you money and say to kiss my ass, you ask where and whether or not I want tongue." He slapped the envelope on the table in front of me. "Now you been paid, do your fucking job."

I shot him five times in the chest. The reports thundered down the corridors of the empty club. The snifter shattered in his hand as his body clenched around the new holes that I'd rudely punched through him. Smoke wisped from the perforated wool jacket just as it curled from his cigarette, somehow still miraculously clutched between the fingers of his other hand. He looked down incredulously at his condition.

"I've already been paid. And I am doing my job. Prick."

"Nguuuuhhhhhhh," Elvis said as he plopped back down onto the leather banquette. It was the smartest thing to come out of his mouth all night.

I picked up the envelope; put it in my own pocket. "Thanks for the tip." With the edge of the tablecloth, I wiped Carlos's prints off the gun and dropped it on the floor. I figured it was only right that I used his piece. It felt like justice that I did. "You never even tried to deny raping the girl, either. That plain ticked me off, just so you know."

And with that, Elvis shuddered once and left the building.

I went to take a leak before I took the drive back to Brooklyn. As I zipped myself up, I took a long stare into the mirror. I didn't look too bad, but I felt older than dust. The three white hairs at my left temple bugged me more than they should have.

Carlos was at an age that I couldn't remember being anymore. I was glad that I got him gone. He didn't need to---

BOOM!

Instinctively, I hit the deck, praying that the janitor had done a good job on the bathroom floor.

Silence.

My heart pounded as I stood, pulling my own gun as I pressed flat against the tile wall. With my free hand, I slowly opened the bathroom door. The club was just as I'd left it. Carlos's gun was still on the floor. Elvis had been considerate enough to stay dead. That meant there was another gun in play other than one in my hand.

"Jesus?" I yelled down the dark hallway.

Nothing

"Jesus, if you're here, give me a heads-up!" I wasn't worried about giving my presence or my position away to the shooter. If whoever it was headed up the corridor, I had him dead-bang.

Still nothing.

Then a pained wail, too high-pitched to be the meaty Dominican.

I pressed myself against the velvet-covered wall and moved slowly towards the cries, gun leading the way. In the dim light over the door, I could make out Jesus, flat on his back in a pool of blood, still clutching his huge revolver. A sizeable piece of his head was squashed in and had split over the ear, a spike of bone jutting out. I assumed that the piece of rebar that lay at his feet had done the job.

I picked up his gun. It must have looked impressive in Jesus' massive paws. Unfortunately for him, all that bulky muscle combined with a handgun too heavy for its own use enabled a high school kid to get the drop on him with a piece of iron.

Carlos was curled against the wall, his wrist tucked under his arm. Blood gushed from his ruined hand. Two of his fingers lay scattered next to Jesus. The shot I heard must have been the one pull of the trigger Jesus got off before his skull collapsed.

Guess Jesus wasn't as good as I'd given him credit for.

Carlos rocked back and forth in pain, not all of it physical. "I killed him. I killed him," he wept.

I knelt down next to him and placed my hand on his back, right between his bony shoulders. "You had to. He would have killed you," I whispered gently. The words were for God to hear as much as they were for him.

"I had to. He would have killed me. He would have killed me," he repeated between gasps. He said the words over and over as though trying to convince himself that they were true. He looked at me. His terrified eyes seeking further consolation in my face, my words.

I shot him once behind the ear. The red Yankees hat flipped off his head as the bullet passed through. Carlos sighed peacefully, then slumped to the carpet.

I put the gun back into Jesus' hand and walked out.

It had started to snow.

I let the heavy knob fall again on the oak door at St. Barbara's Church. I was freezing, the cold of the brass knocker penetrating my leather gloves, but knew Father Ken would eventually open up.

A scowling face under a Celtics hat peered through the door crack as I waved the half bottle. The scowl remained even as he asked, "What's this?" his Dublin lilt dripping with suspicion.

"Frapin. It's cognac." I knew he preferred a good Irish whiskey, but I used what was at hand.

"Any good?"

"Seven hundred dollars a bottle. Retail."

"Only about two hundred left, but I'll take it." He took the bottle from me and I followed him inside. The warm church air was heavy with the ghosts of old incense. The snow was melting into my hair, ice water dripping down my collar. I followed him into the sacristy where he pulled two Dixie cups from the dispenser next to the water cooler. "Will you be joining me?"

"No thanks."

"Still dry, eh?"

"Still dry." Little bit of a lie, but Father Ken didn't need to know that. I put the brakes on just short of drinking myself to death when I realized that the alcohol didn't make my thoughts any cleaner, my demons any quieter. It just got them drunk too. And they were mean drunks.

I still drank slightly more than my annual birthday scotch, but a Dixie cup full of French cognac in a church somehow felt like crossing a line.

Father Ken sighed at the injustice of having to drink alone. He poured himself a double and sipped it gently, rolling it around his tongue. "It's no Jameson's, but it'll do. How many?"

"Four."

Father Ken raised a bushy white eyebrow at me. "Busy night?"

"Bad night."

He opened a drawer and took out four tea candles. "You know where she is. You can let yourself out." He tucked the bottle under his arm and walked back to the dormitory.

I went into the church and made the sign as I passed the cross on my way to her statue.

St. Barbara. The Saint of Gunners.

She was the closest I could find, saint-wise for what I did.

I lit the first candle at St. Barbara's feet for Elvis. As a man, he wasn't worth the match, but his soul needed the candle. I prayed silently.

Underneath my prayer, a voice told me that I had to do what I did. The kid's life was over, one way or the other. There was no way he was going to get away from that point. The place was covered in his blood. His fingers were on the floor, for Christ's sake (sorry). I pushed away the voice and concentrated on who I was specifically praying for.

The second candle was for Jesus. The wrong man at the wrong place at the wrong time, even though he was a bad man and a worse bodyguard. I prayed some more.

The voice came back. I'd saved the kid from an eternity in jail, it said. It said what life remained in him, the State would have ripped out by the time he breathed free air again, if ever.

It was better this way.

For him.

For his family.

It said.

It said.

The third candle was for Carlos. In my prayer, I apologized to him as a lump of guilt filled my throat. I prayed for his forgiveness. The voice told me that I didn't kill him for my own sake.

Because they'd catch him.

Because he'd seen my face.

Because he could then point his remaining fingers at me.

The voice said the words over and over as though trying to convince me that they were true. It said that my act, in the end, was a merciful act.

I lit the last candle for myself.

And prayed as hard as I could.

The Legendary Great Black Cloud of Ralphie O'Malley

"4DC Security," Junior answered the phone in a falsetto about as feminine as Hulk Hogan. Junior had been answering our office phone like that for a good three years running and the joke never seemed to wear on him. He called the voice "Wendy".

Wendy was our imaginary receptionist, which was fine since our imaginary office was a desk stuck in the liquor room above The Cellar, Boston's shittiest rock & roll bar.

I try not to let Junior answer the phone all that much.

I hit the button to turn on the speakerphone just as a weary sigh replied to Wendy's greeting. I recognized the sigh as belonging to Barry Hardon, Boston's lowest of the low-end parole officers. "I don't know why I even call you turkeys."

"Because we work cheap?" I replied.

"Boo, that you?"

"It's me," I answered. Because it was.

"Don't forget me, sexy," Junior said, as Wendy again.

"You're about as sexy as ten-foot catheter."

"Thanks, Hard-On" Junior said in his natural voice, which was somewhere closer to a Rottweiler chewing on gravel.

Barry sighed at the dig, which he'd probably heard at least three times a day during the fifty years he'd been on the planet.

"What've you got for us, Barry?"

Barry sighed again. Seventy to eighty percent of conversation with Barry Hardon consisted of him sighing in various tones and pitches. "I need you guys to go get Ralphie O'Malley again."

"What now?"

"He had a hearing two days ago. Dummy fell asleep drunk on the train. He got picked up for vagrancy.

"Vagrancy? Seriously?"

"Seriously."

"That still a law? The fuck is this, the Great Depression?"

Barry went on. "Kinda. Probably would have gotten it dismissed, if the fuckwit had actually shown up for court."

I swear, only Ralphie O'Malley could get arrested for vagrancy. "We'll have him in by this afternoon. Fee?"

"Two hundred."

"Deal." I hung up the phone.

"How much?" Junior asked.

"Two bills."

"Dammit," he said as he pulled on his coat. "It's fuckin' freezing out. Shoulda got another fifty." Junior pulled knit mittens over his hands. He saw me smirking. "What?"

"Nice mittens, Mary." If you can't see why mittens covering the knuckles of a man with H-A-R-D and C-O-R-E tattooed across them is funny, then I can't explain it to you.

"Hardy-har. You're gonna have a good time explaining to the E.M.T's how these mittens got inside of you."

Ralphie O'Malley always said that his luck permanently switched for the worst on October 2nd, 1978. Ralphie claimed that he was sitting on the lap of the elder Mr. O'Malley the moment Bucky Dent hit his home run out of Fenway. As the ball arced over The Green Monster, Mr. O'Malley leapt up in disbelief, sending Ralphie airborne off the couch and headfirst into the TV screen, effectively busting both the Zenith and his only son's head.

Since that point, society, the fates, and even Ralphie himself considered him something of a jinxed soul—I didn't know of a bar in Boston that didn't eighty-six Ralphie during important baseball games.

Or hockey games.

Or basketball games.

Yeah, Ralphie wasn't much welcome during football season either.

But it was deeper than that. I'd seen some of the old timers actually cross themselves when Ralphie entered the bar, heard people half-kiddingly talk about the invisible cloud of doom that followed him wherever he went.

Remember the Sox in 2004? Everybody thought it was funny to chip in and buy him a weeklong trip to New York during the ALCS.

That jinx ain't so funny any more, is it?

Then there was the night of "the girl".

One evening about two years ago, the heavens parted, the stars aligned and the cloud looked like it lost its way for the night. Lo and behold, Ralphie was talking to a girl. An honest to goodness, living and breathing girl. And a cute little blonde, at that.

Silently, we all rooted him on. We'd never seen him talking to a girl before. All seemed to be going well. I even thought I might have even seen a twirl of the hair.

Then the cloud found its way back to Ralphie's coordinates.

Out of nowhere, somebody dropped a full pitcher of beer from the balcony. It wasn't heavy, just angled right. The pitcher landed right on the crown of Ralphie's head, knocking him silly. The cheap beer erupted in a mushroom cloud, directly into the blonde's face. Ralphie was lights-out for less than a minute, but of course by that time the girl had skedaddled in beer-soaked humiliation.

Now, for most people, embarrassing as that incident might have been, the story would have made for a great bar tale of ill-fate and circumstance, told over and over to great guffaws and shots of whiskey lifted in good humor. For Ralphie, it was just another bitch-slap from the heavens. Hell, even Junior and me couldn't find the funny in his tragi-comic existence anymore, and we're the masters of the form. Most of the time, it was just sad.

"Warming up" Junior's car was just a figure of speech, since the heater didn't work. It was also three below zero that afternoon. Wind chill my ass. Cold is cold. We sat there, shivering and cupping our hands over our cigarette cherries for warmth while Junior's '79 Buick, (which for some sweet fuck-all reason he'd named Ms. Kitty), slowly stopped coughing like a habitual three-packer.

"You gotta get this heater fixed, Junior." My demand might have had more weight if Ms. Kitty's heater had ever worked.

Junior glared at me, then tenderly rubbed the dashboard, as if I might have injured the car's feelings.

We drove onto Storrow Dive heading out to Quincy, where Ralphie lived in a house with his mother.

Miss Kitty had warmed up to a temperature just above welldigger's arse by the time we got to the O'Malley residence. If houses were representative of the people who lived in them, then Ralphie's was dead-on. The paint might have been light blue at one point, but had faded into a peeling gray, hanging off of the weather-beaten shingles for dear life. The porch, half-built, had never been painted at all—a project undertaken long ago and never finished. It too, looked like it was clinging to the house simply because it had no better place to be.

Junior clucked his tongue as he killed the ignition. "This is gonna break Mrs. O'Malley's heart again." Miss Kitty wheezed once in seeming agreement, then fell silent.

"You'd think she'd be used to it by now."

"Wonder what she cooked last night?"

It wasn't the first time we'd had to pick up Ralphie. Almost a year ago, Ralphie got busted for public drunkenness after he peed, blind drunk, between two parked cars. One of the parked cars just happened to be an idling black-and-white.

When we showed up at the O'Malley house the last time Ralphie forgot he had a court date, Mrs. O'Malley cooked us leftovers while Ralphie showered and got dressed. She cried the whole time. That alone might have been enough to kill the appetite of lesser men, but Mrs. O'Malley made one hell of a chicken pot pie. Besides, it seemed to make her feel better to be doing something just then, to feel appreciated. As far as I could tell, Ralphie never disrespected his mother, just took her for granted like a lot of people do with their parents.

Junior and I both lost our families when we were kids. For a long time growing up, all we had was each other. We knew how important family was. And how fragile. We appreciated a warm meal from a mother—even if it wasn't our own—in ways you wouldn't understand if you still have yours around. Appreciate those pot pies.

The front steps groaned under our weight, as if they too were dreading our presence. The wind blew cold whips across the porch and our faces. All of a sudden, I found myself coveting Junior's mittens. "Ring the bell."

"You ring the bell."

"I'll ring the bell, but you're telling her."

"Hell with that. Ralphie's telling her."

"What if Ralphie isn't here? We have to tell her something."

Junior either shrugged or was wracked by a huge shiver. "Tell her we came here for a play date."

"Just for being stupid, you get to ring the bell. Please, before something freezes off of me."

"Bet you wish you had mittens now, don't ya?"

As Junior and I bandied our Mensa-level discourse back and forth, the front door swung open. I had a half-second to assume that somebody heard us coming up the steps. I say "half-second" because during the latter half, an arm clutching what looked like a wooden blackjack with a leather strap came crashing down into the middle of Junior's face. Blood sprayed from his nostrils as he lurched back, stepped on a slick of ice, and went tumbling backwards down the porch steps. Lord, it looked painful.

I took a step back from our attacker and got ready to crack somebody's skull with a straight right. Then I found myself face to face with all five-feet, two-inches of Mrs. O'Malley. Complete with pink and orange floral print housedress on.

And one shoe off.

She was wild eyed, panicked. "You leave my Ralphie alone!" she shrieked. She raised her weapon again, ready to brain me with it this time. "Don't you hurt him anymore!"

"MrsO'MalleyMrsO'Malley!!!" I leapt back, hands up defensively. "It's just us! It's Boo and Junior!

She squinted at me through lenses thicker than those used on the Hubble, but kept her hand up. It was then that I saw her weapon. It was her other shoe. She'd attacked us with one of her wooden orthopedic sandals. "Boo?"

"Yes, ma'am," I said. My hands were trembling, part adrenaline rush and part hypothermia.

"Baaah-bra?" Came a voice from across the street. In the doorway facing opposite us, another housedress was standing with a steaming cup of Dunkin Donuts coffee in one hand and a cigarette in the other. "You want me to cawl the cahps?" she yowled. Neighborly help with a Boston accent thicker than paste.

"We're fine!" I yelled back and returned my attention to Mrs. O'Malley. "We're not here to hurt Ralphie." Then I noticed that her trembling lower lip was pooched out and bloodied. Somebody had popped her one. And recently.

"I'm nawt asking you!" from across the street.

"Junior?" she asked the crumpled heap lying upside-down on her front steps.

"Guhhhhh," replied Junior.

We sat in the dining room while Mrs. O'Malley reheated some chowder and biscuits for us. Junior had a black garbage bag with ice in it pressed against his nose. The long remainder of the bag trailed up and over his head like a novelty plastic wig.

"You look like the worlds worst Cher impersonator."

"I'll make *you* Cher," he threatened.

I took a second. "What?"

"Shaddup. Look at me!" He lowered the bag. "Excuse me if my comebacks ain't up to par today, dickweed." His nose, obviously broken, had taken the shape and color of a small eggplant. Just above his pathetic honker sat an ugly bump with a scabbing scrape along it.

Mrs. O'Malley waddled back into the small dining area balancing two huge bowls of soup and a Tupperware container between them. "I'm so sorry I hit you, Junior. I thought you were those other men."

"What other men?" I asked through a mouthful of biscuit.

"The big men who came and took my Ralphie away." Tears welled behind her glasses, the moisture making her eyes look like two bloodshot fishbowls.

Junior and I looked at each other over our bowls. "They say who they worked for?" Junior asked between spoonfuls.

"No, they just said that they were coming to get him. That he was late."

Goddamn you Barry, I thought. "What did they look like?"

"One was big and had blonde hair the other one was heavyset and bald. The bald one hit me." She pointed at her fat lip.

I looked at Junior again, his mouth pursed tight in the same anger I felt. We knew the grabbers. The Swede and Fat Pat. Two other meatballs for hire, both of whom had brief stints under us at 4DC. We fired the Swede for being stupid.

Let me tell you, when a man is fired from a bouncing job for being stupid, that says something. He couldn't figure out how to subtract 21 years from the driver's licenses. One too many requests for Lady Googoo (or whatever the fuck her name is) on the jukebox was what clued us off that our clientele had taken a sudden dip in the age bracket.

Fat Pat was just a mean pituitary case who had the misfortune of being fat and having been named Pat. Calling him heavyset was the charity of the year. Fat Pat looked like a pink Irish blimp.

"We'll find Ralphie for you, Mrs. O'Malley. We promise."

She smiled and sniffed back her tears. "You boys really don't have to. I know my Ralphie can get himself into trouble. It's not your problem. He just breaks my heart sometimes."

"It's not a problem. We want to make sure he's all right too."

She squeezed my shoulder with a pudgy hand. "Let me get you boys some cheesecake," she said, and headed back to the kitchen.

Junior glared at me.

"What? I got chowder on my face?" I dabbed at my chin with the holiday print paper towels we were using as napkins.

"What did you promise that for? Isn't this more than enough work for two hundred dollars? Two hundred dollars that we ain't even gonna get now?"

"C'mon, Junior. She's old, she's alone, and she's scared. We're just going to make sure that those two fucktards brought Ralphie to Barry and didn't put him in the hospital."

"If they'da showed up with Ralphie already, Hard-On wouldn't have called us."

"That's my point."

Junior folded his arms across his chest. "I just can't believe you promised her. Never promise anything to nobody."

"What if I promise to love you forever?"

"Touch me and I kill you."

"Homophobe."

"I'm a you-aphobe." And before I could mock his poor comeback, "Fuck off."

"Thanks Barry, you colossal prick," I said as we stormed into his office.

"Hey. Hey!" Barry held his arms out, indicating his office and the man sitting across from his desk. "I'm with a client here!"

"Hey George," I said to his client.

"Hey Boo."

"What's the big idea sending Swede and Fat Pat over before us?" Junior sat on the edge of the desk and ruffled around the papers on the blotter. "That's not very professional of you, sending two teams on the same job."

"What?"

"Your little brother again?" I asked George.

"Yeah. Stupid-ass kid stole a car this time."

"He eighteen yet?"

"Turned last week."

"That's no good."

"You're telling me. What happened to his nose?" George swirled a finger in the general direction of Junior's ugliness.

"Got hit with a shoe."

"Oh"

"Cut it out!" Barry stood and slammed his palms onto the papers that Junior was mussing. "What the fuck is the matter with you two?"

I glared at him. "Why did you send Fat Pat and The Swede to the O'Malley's before us? We're not your fucking clean-up crew."

"First of all, they're idiots." Junior tipped over Barry's pencil holder. Pens clattered onto the floor."

Barry groaned and sighed, "Now look what you did." Then he shook his head, confused at my accusation. "Who's an idiot?"

"Secondly, did Fat Pat tell you he socked an old lady in the mouth in the process?"

Junior was reaching for the coffee cup that read World's Greatest Grandpa when Barry stabbed at his hand with a letter opener, missing his fingers by an inch. The opener stuck straight into the worn wood. "You touch one more thing Junior, and I swear to God I'll stick your hand to the desk."

Barry pried the opener from the desk and held it stomach-level to keep us at bay. "Now. Calm down." Barry smoothed his thin hair, composing himself after our mess-up attack. "Mr. Smart, would you please wait in the front room while we sort this thing out?"

George crossed his legs and leaned back into the fake leather chair. "Nah, I'd rather hear what these guys have to say."

"Yeah Hard-On. Let him hear about the kinds of guys you're hiring now to do your pick-ups."

"What guys? I hired you two jackasses. Where's Ralphie?"

"You tell us."

Barry's face was a shifting mass of bewilderment and twitching eyelids. He held his hands up, palms open, and breathed deeply through his nostrils. It whistled like a tiny tea kettle. "Now," he said through clenched teeth and forced composure, "why would I know where Ralphie is? Isn't that what I hired you two numbnuts to figure out?"

"So your first team never brought him in? That what you're saying?"

"You are the first fucking team!" Barry hollered. He held his palms up again, re-composing. His tea kettle nose whistled once more as he took another deep, calming breath. Then he opened up the drawer of the desk, popped two antacids and chased it with Maalox. Calmly, he said "You don't have Ralphie then. Is that what you're telling me?"

Junior sucked on his teeth. "Uh. No."

I said, "You don't have him either?"

"I do not."

"Shit,"

Barry sighed into one of his trademark groans. "So what you're telling me is, somebody else got him before you two did?"

"Looks that way."

"Who?"

"Well, we know who. Now we have to figure out why."

"Well, why don't you both do that. Because one drawer down? Under the one filled with pills and syrups to keep me from hemorrhaging myself into the morgue every time I sit on the crapper?"

"Yeah?"

"I have a gun."

"Gotcha," we both said at the same time.

"Always good to see you George," I said as I backed out of the office.

"Yeah. Better circumstances next time, huh?"

Junior was slowly backing out, too. "Yeah. Forget everything we said. Barry's a great guy."

"Real stand-up," I said.

"For a Hard-On."

Barry reached for the drawer. We ran like hell.

By the time we got back to the car, Mother Nature had decided to take a swipe at us too. Ominous black clouds roiled over the Boston skyline, the air holding the charge of an impending storm

"Well, ain't that just a dandy," Junior said, flinging his hands skyward in frustration. "So now what? I'd say we got maybe a couple of hours before we get dumped on."

"You hear how much we're getting?"

"Yeah. Two hundred dollars for this bullshit."

"I was talking about snow."

"I know what you were talking about."

"Maybe there's something back at the O'Malley's. Other that that, we just have to find Fat Pat or Swede."

"If the snow doesn't cover them up, we might be able to find a trail of fried chicken bones. That should lead us to Pat, at least."

"Do we have their numbers still?"

"What? You gonna call them and ask; 'Hey, you guys beat Ralphie O'Malley into a coma?', or do you have another question in mind?"

"Bring the mountain to Mohammed, my brother. We'll call them and say we need extra guys for a gig."

"Think they'll buy it? Fat Pat sure as shit qualifies as a mountain."

"They should. They're even dumber than us."

"True dat."

Back at The Cellar, Junior and I waited downstairs where the bands played. It was early enough in the day that the space was still completely empty.

Did I mentioned it was soundproofed?

Half an hour after I left a message on The Swede's voicemail, I could hear the huge, thumping footfalls that heralded Fat Pat's march down the stairs.

I crouched behind the gate opposite the entryway. They walked in, looking around for us in the darkened room, the only light emanating from the red exit signs.

"Where are they?" Fat Pat wheezed softly from the exertion of walking down a flight of stairs.

"What time they say to be here?" asked Swede.

I shut the gate with a slam, making them both jump in surprise. Well, Pat didn't jump exactly, but he did wiggle.

"Jesus, Boo," wheezed Fat Pat.

Behind them, Junior silently vaulted the bar, baseball hat in hand.

The Swede caught a glint of metal reflecting off my hand. Dumbly, he asked, "Why you wearing knuckles, Boo?"

Junior swung for the fences, whacking the bat into the thick meat at the back of Fat Pat's thighs. Fat Pat screamed, dropping hard to his knees onto the concrete floor. With Pat's weight behind it, the fall probably hurt more than the bat.

The Swede turned to his fallen buddy. I could almost smell his synapses firing. "Hey!"

I socked him hard in the ribs with the brass knuckles. With a pained explosion of breath, Swede was on the ground next to his pet blob.

I flicked the lights on and stood over the two dummies. "Now, before this experience gets any more painful for you guys, just tell us who told you to grab Ralphie O'Malley and...what the fuck happened to your head, Swede?"

Swede had a huge purple shiner, the whites turned blood-red from smashed blood vessels. Over the eye, a huge red knot bulged horribly. More than slightly ashamed, The Swede said, "I got hit with a shoe."

Junior and I looked at each other. "No shit?"

"No shit," Swede said. "What happened to your nose, Junior?"

"That woman is a fuckin' menace," Fat Pat said, shifting uncomfortably in his barstool. His legs must have still hurt like a motherfucker. Boo-hoo. Since it took the three of us to help Fat Pat back up the stairs, my back was killing me. I drew the short straw and got bottom duty while Junior and The Swede pulled from above. I'd have to remember to boil my hands after.

"She's like Bruce Lee with a Dr. Sholl," Junior agreed nasally, his nose clogged from the swelling.

"It was an accident. I mean, I swung on her, but I didn't know who was hitting at us when I did. She's a freakin' animal."

The Swede gingerly touched his disgusting eye. "But we swear to God, Boo. We never hurt Ralphie. We just grabbed him for--"

Fat Pat silenced him with a hard glare.

"For who?" I asked.

"We don't know," Fat Pat said, a bit too quickly. "We got an anonymous call, said pick up Ralphie."

"Who paid you, then?"

"Direct deposit." Fat Pat said, then smiled, obviously satisfied with his on-the-fly answer. Truth be told, it was pretty smart for Fat Pat.

"Where did you drop him then?"

"I…" I reached over and grabbed a fistful of Fat Pat's ear and twisted. *"Ow-ow-oww!"* he whined.

I loosened the twist but didn't let go. "Shut it. I'm asking Swede." While Fat Pat may have exhibited a minor talent for improvisation, Swede was dumber than a bag of wet hamsters.

Swede looked nervously at Fat Pat. "We… Just… Dropped him off?" He answered in the form of a question, like an unsure fifth-grader. But since this wasn't Jeopardy, I continued my line of interrogation.

"Where?"

"On a corner?"

"Let me get this straight," Junior interjected. "You two rocket scientists snatched Ralphie, then just released him back into the wild on some corner? Is that what you're babbling at us Swede?"

"Yes."

"Retard," Fat Pat muttered.

"Hoooo-kay, Pat," I sighed, "as much a contradiction in terms as this may be, natural order has made you the brains of your operation. Swede?"

"Yeah."

"You're a retard. Fuck off."

"Got it." Swede jumped up and walked out quickly, abandoning Pat. He stopped at the doorway. "Yo Pat. Call me later if you want to rent a movie or somethin'."

"I'm gonna step on your head later, is what I'm gonna do, you stupid fuck."

The Swede looked sincerely hurt by Fat Pat's anger and walked away, head down. I felt a twinge of guilt, like I'd just kicked a disabled puppy.

I turned my attention back to Pat. "So, all things considered, we're just going to keep hurting you until you tell us who paid you to get Ralphie." I twisted his ear again.

Pat squealed in pain. "I can't," he whined.

Junior leaned in close. "Whaddaya think, Boo? Another inch and the ear starts to tear off?"

"Let's see."

"Garrett!" Fat Pat shrieked. "We took him to Al Garrett!"

"Aw, no," Junior said softly.

I released his ear and smacked him upside the head with the same hand. "What's wrong with you?"

"He paid us."

"How much?" Asked Junior.

"Five hundred."

Junior leveled his gaze at me. "More than we're getting."

"We don't do work for that psycho."

"Just saying."

"Where did you drop him?"

"The Garrett Bowl."

Albert Garrett ran a vast bookmaking operation out of a bowling alley in North Quincy. Word had it that he and his crew of townie goons used the bowling balls and pins with a great deal of creativity to hurt people who were late with his money. I don't even want to talk about the ball-polisher rumor.

I did, however, want to beat the cellulite off of Pat, but instead said, "Get the fuck out of here," in a tone that left no room for misinterpretation of what the day held for him if he stayed.

Never has four-hundred pounds moved so fast. He looked like a Beluga ninja as he shot out the door.

"Now what?" Junior asked.

I groaned and rubbed the tension spot between my eyes. "Feel like driving out to Quincy?"

"No, but I guess we kinda have to now, don't we?"

"Yeah."

"I'm just glad you didn't try to get all clever and said something like 'Let's go bowling'."

"Shut up."

Momentum and element of surprise count for a lot, but a full charge in a car battery counts for something too. About a half a mile from the bowling alley, Miss Kitty decided to cough and wheeze herself to a sputter just as the first thick clumps of snow started tumbling from the sky. I melted a few on the way down with the fiery language that I directed at the car and Junior.

There went our momentum.

Ever try to muscle a small tank through the snow? Then you'd know what it was like trying to move a '79 Buick through a Nor'easter. If we didn't find a gas station soon, we'd have a real problem on our hands. Junior seemed calmly unsurprised.

"You knew this would happen, didn't you," I asked as I pushed from inside the passenger door. My calves burned with the effort.

"Sooner or later. The catalytic converter is jacked."

"And you haven't fixed it...why?"

"Because we don't make me enough money for these stupid fucking gigs that leave us stranded in a fucking blizzard?"

'Nuff said.

Of course, the next gas station was directly across the street from the alley. Junior popped the hood and then the trunk. He pulled another battery from the boot.

"You had another battery in there the whole time?"

"This one's not juiced either."

"Why?"

"I just keep switching and re-charging the batteries when I need to. Forgot to juice both."

I was about to nail Junior with a vicious retort, but couldn't squeeze it out between my chattering teeth. That was our lives, in a nutshell. Jury-rigged. Held together with tape and twine and a whole lot of duct tape.

Then it hit me...

If the grapevine held true about Al Garrett, we might have a card to play after all.

"Junior, wait." I grabbed his shoulder as he headed into the garage.

"What?"

"I got an idea. I need that battery."

I went into Junior's trunk. It was the usual treasure trove of worthless shit. I pulled some wires from a busted receiver (that he'd been meaning to get fixed), a joystick from an old Nintendo (he didn't know why he had it) and of course, duct tape. I stuffed the contraption into a grease-stained duffel bag and told him my plan.

Junior grinned and nodded appreciably. "Fuckin' MacGuyver."

Fuckin' MacGuyver.

The four goons stopped their bowling game when Junior and I walked through the frosted glass doors of The Garrett Bowl. I never realized how eerie a silent bowling alley was. You could've heard a mouse fart as the goons watched us walking through the lobby.

We went up to the bored-looking girl behind the shoe rental booth. I could smell her hairspray across the counter. Her bangs saluted us crisply. She didn't look up from her nail filing when I cleared my throat. Probably for the better. Junior didn't look up from the ten-grand worth of cleavage that heaved between her open-collared bowing shirt.

She popped her gum. "You guys Boo and Junior?"

Shit.

And there went the element of surprise.

"Um. Yeah."

"Al's waiting for you." She pointed a pink talon at the door next to the counter that read: Manager's Office.

Allow me to reiterate.

Shit.

We opened the door and walked in to see the wide back of a black leather chair. A finger came up from the other side, giving us the 'one minute'. Garrett was on the phone. "Yeah. The line is four and a half, you give him seven. The numbnuts is so in love with the Pats, he'd do it on nine. Yeah..."

The rumors were true. Behind the desk were a dozen flat-screen TV's, each one broadcasting a different sporting event; from the greyhounds at Wonderland Park to a poker tournament to—was he watching cricket? On the desk sat three expensive-looking computer banks, complete with three more flat-screen monitors.

He'd come a long way since his old man ran afoul of a chest full of cholesterol and left the bookie business to little Al. Twenty-five years old at the time, everybody laughed when the skinny kid went to collect on his dead old man's vigs. Al answered the dismissals with a brutality that became its own urban legend, stories that degenerate gamblers tell their kids to get them to eat their peas.

A decade later, nobody was laughing any more. Not after the rumors about the ball-polisher hit the grapevine.

"Call me tomorrow." He finished his conversation and turned his chair to us. Al Garrett looked a lot younger than his current thirty-five years. His long hair was slicked back and tied behind the navy suit jacket that looked like it cost more than my entire wardrobe. That wasn't saying much, since my entire wardrobe was probably worth about sixteen bucks. The suit was nice, nevertheless.

"You're Boo and Junior, right?"

"I'm Boo," I said, stupidly.

"I'm Junior," Junior said unnecessarily.

"How did you know we were coming?"

"When Tom Brady's nuts itch, I know how hard he scratches. You think I wouldn't know that you two assholes were coming my way?"

I made a mental note to have a serous conversation with Fat Pat the next time I ran into him.

Junior bunched his fists. Garrett saw it. "Unh, uh, uh." He waggled his fingers and the huge canary diamond on his manicured pinkie finger twinkled at us. I wondered if the girl in the lobby did his nails for him. "You don't want to pull any tough guy horseshit with me, boys." The finger moved under the desk. "I press this little button underneath here and those four big guys out there come running in. I'm afraid they're not very nice."

Neither were we. If Garrett's bruisers were on a par with Fat Pat and Swede, I think we'd normally have had a righteous chance. Unfortunately, Junior and I were both half-frozen and spent from pushing a goddamn Buick for a mile and a half. As it was, I gave us a fifty-fifty chance, at best.

"We're not here to start shit. We were just wondering how business was," I said.

Garrett smiled crookedly at me, opening his arms to encompass his obviously pricey electronic kingdom. "Not bad," he said, dripping sarcasm.

"Then why are you fucking with small fries like Ralphie O'Malley?"

The smug little bastard steepled his fingers on the desk. "Let me explain something to you guys about business. I'm working with a lot of figures here. Am I going to bust up somebody who owes me fifty G's and make him incapable of working and earning my money? Or am I going to bust up the guy that owes me five and make sure that Mr. Fifty gets a clear picture of his future?"

His point made perfect sense to me, which made me a little ill. "We just want to know where Ralphie is. Beyond that, we don't have any stake in this."

Garrett leaned his chin onto his hands. "Now, why would I tell you anything if you have no stake in it? That wouldn't be very good business, would it?" He bit his lower lip coyly. "Tell you what. You give me the five grand that Ralphie owes me, and I'll tell you where that fucking loser wound up."

I reached into the bag and pulled out my contraption. Garrett went eight shades of sickened gray and reached under the desk.

"Unh, uh, uh," Junior said, waggling his finger this time. "Why don't you keep those pretty rings where we can see them, Zsa Zsa."

He slapped his hands quickly onto the desktop.

I pressed a button on the joystick. "If your hands move, I press that button again. Then you have a serious problem."

Garrett's color settled on a nice shade of green. "Are you guys fucking nuts? You're threatening me with a bomb?"

Junior and I laughed. "Why would we do that? This isn't a bomb. Like I said, we don't have a stake in this. But right now, you sure as shit do."

Some pink returned to Garrett's face. "Then what in Christ's name--"

"It's an industrial-grade electromagnet. Amazing what a little knowhow and a helpful nerd at Radio Shack can accomplish."

Green all over again, Garrett made a soft choking noise deep in his throat.

Junior circled his finger teasingly over the red joystick button on our car battery Frankenstein. "So, if you move your hand, we activate this sucker and wipe out all the electronics in the building."

"Though I'm sure that smart-boy here has backed up all his numbers, addresses and amounts onto another system." I looked at Garrett and grinned. "Right?"

He made that moist choking sound again.

Junior tapped a thoughtful finger over his lip. "I'm even willing to bet it'll conk out that panic alarm of his, which should give us plenty of quiet time to beat both the crap and the whereabouts of Ralphie out of you."

Garrett cleared his throat. Greasy sweat poured down his greasy forehead. "If you press that button, or lay a hand on me, I swear to God you will one day find out what your own cock tastes like."

"You tried that once, didn't you Junior?"

"I was young. I was experimenting."

"You get close?"

"Meh. Couple more yoga classes and I'd have had it."

"You two clowns think I'm kidding?" He was talking tough, but his hands were still pressed to the desktop.

"Albert, Albert, Albert," I sat on the corner of his desk," do you really want to get into that kind of mess, cock removal, forced ingestion of removed cocks, etc, etc, over little Ralphie O'Malley?"

A droplet of sweat dangled on Garrett's nose. He closed his eyes and inhaled deeply. Beaten, he said, "I had him dropped off at his house five hours ago."

"What?"

"I don't have him. You're right. You think that little shit is worth me getting into anything serious? I had the boys slap him around, then dropped him off at his mama's around two this afternoon."

A little light bulb popped on over my head. The only thing it illuminated was how stupid we'd been. "Well, been nice doing business with you."

Junior packed up our battery and we walked out the door.

All that for nothing. At least Garrett hadn't called our bluff. Our "industrial-grade electromagnet" couldn't even start an old Buick, much less demagnetize anything.

MacGuyver, my ass.

"You've got to be fuckin' kidding me," Junior said as Miss Kitty fishtailed through the rising snow. A small snow bank passed dangerously close to my door. We couldn't afford to get stuck now.

It was there all along.

We were so taken aback by Mrs. O'Malley's kamikaze shoe attack that we didn't listen close enough to what she was saying. She'd said, "leave my Ralphie alone," And "don't hurt him anymore." Who was she protecting if Ralphie wasn't there? If he hadn't been returned, how could she have known that he'd been hurt?

We got played big time by a sweet old lady.

God dammit.

Visibility was nearing zero when we pulled up in front of the O'Malley residence for the second time that day. A set of fading footprints leading away from the house were freshly marked in the snow.

Junior squatted over the prints. "You think Ralphie bolted?"

I shook my head. "Those are Mrs. O'Malley's shoes. Feet are too small, and look..." Edged around the first few steps in the snow were ruby flakes of what was probably Junior's blood.

"Small feet, my ass." Junior cupped his busted nose. "Where the hell is she going in this shit?"

"Probably ran to Star Market for some blizzard supplies." I felt a twinge of sadness at the thought of the old woman trudging through the snow in her sandals, felt bad for eating her food. Looking at the sad house, I realized for the first time just how little she and Ralphie had other than that depressing piece of real estate and each other.

We didn't want to bust open Mrs. O'Malley's door, despite her lies and assault, so we tried a couple of the ground floor windows. All locked of course. Junior looked up at the second level. "There we go."

Craning my neck, I could barely make out the tip of a blue curtain billowing through a cracked window jamb.

"Bend over," I said. We had to move fast, my fingers were starting to go numb again in the cold.

"Now's not the time, Brokeback."

"Cut the shit. We got to hurry before Mrs. O'Malley gets back. Let me climb on you. I think I can reach the ledge of the lower roof."

"No way. Lemme climb on your back."

"Are you kidding? You way thirty pounds more than me. Besides, my arms are longer. Or do you want to wait it out and dance with Dr. Scholl again?"

Junior muttered something about his goddamn jacket, but bent over. I climbed on his back and had to stand on my toes to reach the ledge. Junior howled as my toes dug into his spine. My fingers grasped around the edge just as Junior disappeared from under my feet, cursing all things about me. I swung my right leg up and over the lip, but couldn't get enough purchase in the driving snow to bring my left leg up.

"Pull, you tubby bastard," Junior yelled from below.

I swear to God…

I had one shot to grab the sill and pull myself up. If I missed, I was going back over the edge. That thick Irish fuck had better catch me.

I let go of the gutter and scrambled for the window. I started to slide when my fingers caught the jamb and held.

From across the street, I heard, "Hey! You stawp that! I'm cawlin' the cawps!"

Housecoat was back.

"Better move, brudda," yelled Junior. "I think she means it this time."

I was too out of breath to answer, but figured we had a few minutes until the cops could respond, blizzard and all.

I pulled myself up and opened the window wide enough to climb into. One leg was in before my other foot slipped in the snow. I toppled through the opening and landed in a heap onto the floor, the wind knocked out of me on impact.

I lay in that heap wheezing for a few seconds, staring at the wall of the room that I'd belly-flopped into.

Unless Mrs. O'Malley hung a decades-old Jim Rice poster in her bedroom, I'd climbed right into Ralphie's room. With more effort than I thought would be necessary, I managed to get to my feet. All things considered, I was feeling pretty good about my athletic abilities when I saw what was on the bed.

"Aw, hell no," I whispered to the nobody else in the room.

Junior's teeth chattered ferociously when I opened the front door for him. "The fuck, Malone? You stop to take a shit?" Then he got a look at my face. "What? What is it?"

I led him up the stairs into Ralphie's room.

Ralphie lay on the bed. A black garbage bag, just like the one Junior had on his nose earlier, was still pressed to his head. The draping plastic looked as though the legendary Great Black Cloud of Ralphie O'Malley had descended right onto his face. As I pulled the bag away, the condensation from the melting ice rained down his face like tears.

"Fuuuuuuuck… He's dead, isn't he?"

"Yeah." I said.

"Those motherfuckers..."

Ralphie had been worked over pretty hard. His eye was swollen shut and crusted blood still clung in his nostrils.

But they didn't kill him.

I turned Ralphie's head so Junior could see what I'd already seen.

Caked blood had trickled out his ear and matted into the ratty pillowcase. The left side of his face was dented deep, a clear indentation on his temple.

An indentation that was the same size and shape of an orthopedic shoe heel.

"Fuck me with a chainsaw," Junior said, as sadly as a man can say 'fuck me with a chainsaw.'

The sound of locks tumbling snapped us both back to attention. We heard the front door open.

"Ralphie? I'm home. They were out of Devil Dogs, but I got you some Ring Dings."

Junior and I just stood there looking at one another, as frozen and silent as Ralphie.

"Ralphie?" she called again. I could hear tears in her voice. "I'm sorry, honey. Please talk to me. I'm sorry I hit you." The tears turned into guilt-ridden wails. "We'll get the money somehow. Please, Ralphie. You gotta stop gambling." Deep, wracking sobs echoed up the stairwell at us. "Ralphie, please talk to me..."

My heart broke on her every word. Junior bit his lower lip and shook his head. We'd heard enough. I unlocked the deadbolt on Ralphie's door and opened it. "Mrs. O'Malley?" I yelled.

"Who is that?" Fear overtook her sorrow for the moment.

"It's Boo and Junior, ma'am. You have to call a doctor. I think Ralphie's really hurt."

Junior punched me on the arm. "What are you saying to her, Boo? He ain't hurt, he's fuckin' dead."

"You want to tell her?" I hissed.

He bit his lip again.

"What's wrong with Ralphie?" Panic edged her voice.

"Mrs. O'Malley?" I said, as I descended the stairs. She stood shaking in the foyer, looking very small and very cold. "He needs an ambulance," was all I could say.

We sat with her and held her hand until the police arrived.

Acknowledgements, Thank-Yous and a Bunch of Bullshit That Nobody Really Reads Except For People Trying to Find Their Own Name

First of all, thanks to the magazines and anthologies that have published my fiction over the years. You would be: *Plots With Guns*, *Needle Magazine*, *Shotgun Honey*, *Strange, Weird, and Wonderful*, *Out of the Gutter*, *Pulp Pusher*, *Grift*, *Demolition Magazine* and *CrimeFactory*. You guys have great taste.

Then there's my agent, Stacia Decker. She's the agent we all hope to get someday when we type our first words onto paper. You kill it, even though I haven't earned you a red goddamn cent yet. Soon. I promise (wink).

To my family. I love you, but you have no one to blame but yourselves. You made me this way.

My wife and son; Allison? Sam? You guys are why I do it all.

And in case you enjoyed the stories here, follow me on Twitter @bigdaddythug for insane ramblings, new short story updates and my opinions an all kinds of bullshit.

Till next time...Todd Robinson 04/23/2012